CALIF of FORNIA

PAT'RICK NEAL PUGH

PNP
Reseda, California

©1992 by Pat´rick Neal Pugh
All Rights Reserved.

Library of Congress Catalog Number:
93-92578

ISBN: 1-883184-08-8

Manufactured in the United States of America.

First Paperback Edition: June 1993

Published by **P**$_\textbf{N}$**P**
Reseda, California

This book is dedicated
to the real Haggard Woman,
not Shewn,
           Shaun.

also by the author...

Sword Dance Of The Generalissimos

Poet Tree Poof!

Cuisine Is Poetry

Contents ~

1	USHERANCE OF A MISBEGOTTEN MONK	1
2	THE THREE GODS	23
3	ANGELS OF THE AIRT	41
4	BEFORE THE FALL	57
5	BICCH OF THE BIBLIOWERMIN	63
6	THE FEATHERWEIGHT AND THE RAVEN	77
7	SALMON RUSH TO DIE	87
8	THE GRASSY KNOLL	93
9	THE CROWKEEPERS' CROFT	101
10	THE WINDY WAY	107
11	NIGHT ON THE STUMP STOOL	115
12	THE HAGGARD WOMAN AND THE RAINBOW MAN	129
13	CIRCLE OF PURPLE	147
14	THE LOST SUPPER	159
15	CEREMENT ON THE MOUNT	171
16	QUEAN OF THE OBLONG VALLEY	179
17	BATTLE IN THE COW PATTIES	189
18	CALIF OF FORNIA	203

1
USHERANCE OF A MISBEGOTTEN MONK

My lot was a life at sea
Until I came across
The lighthouse
Of a candle-flame.
Yea, I ran aground
When I found
The Book.
Nothing wooden
Would ever be the same.
*   amen.*

Fictionairy

Pollenesia < as in sneezæ
The First Crossing < one before The 2nd Coming (?!)
Swishswooshswashswoosh < the sound one hears when sticking one's head out of a porthole just above the waterline when a ship is hightailing away from harbor
Dragonship < ship with smokestack(s)
Antiphons < arguable As to Qs (?)
Skepsis < a skeptical word
Spid < spider without an *er*
Weald < a field of forest
Layfra < 1. an unnecessary escapist who found a sanctuary 2. a necessary escapist found in an asylum 3. a lay bro
Cacography < opposite of calligraphy
Hermeneutists < 1. *'science!'* of reading 'tween lines instead of writing one's own 2. plural of one who puts words in another's authorship
Caliginous < not an obscure Caesar forgotten before The Fall; obscure in the Archaic
Poetesques < poetry in Poet-talk
Handuscript < manuscript on wood, wood-burned by hand but not handwritten
Erotemes < plural: marks of interrogation ???
Picapicaticatica < a typewriter 'talking'

Every seafarer knows that where certain casts of clouds loom on the midocean horize, mystic isles arise. These sea pyramides, shiftless as driftwood, oasis the aquamarine desert. Exotic whiffs ~ palm frond perfume ~ emanate from these unmappable sea-mounds. The flowery fragrances, reminiscent of a bygone era of luscious innocence, remind us of the paradisiac archipelago of Pollenesia ~ that fabled lei of hopping isles not Xed nor charted properly since The First Crossing.

Hula-hula, poopoo! Cloud-skirted floating sea lands abloom with the incense of lush redolence ~ haha, tehehehe!!! Sound like bosh sandwich dished up with a poi dip? Nonsense is not on the menu. Those of us who have peered thru the oxeye portholes of crew quarters ~ nostrils aflame with malodorous insult, crude vapors of fuel oil and other poisonous foeters ~ *we* know better. As sure as the oars of modern slave galleys are hidden below the waterline, beaten in tune by the swishswooshswashswoosh of lashing pirate tides, floating isles crisscross the dragonship prowbreaks and wakes out on the open seasaw.

Before a harbor kirk's altar, even in an amicable dockside tavern, erstwhile harpooners would sooner arm wrestle or Christcross my allegation as sworn testimonial gospel rather than swab schooners. Cross my bones, toss my toredo-eaten skull to the gulls: as certain as floebergs iceland the Borealis and Australis foams, tropical isles surf on the warmer barm of the Torrid breakers.

Verily, one need not be an old salt-tar of the Sinbad seas, nor long on this earth, to behold other wonderous and flighty isles defying the ponderance of *Science!*

Science! ~ the varment of naupathiac vomit ~ the *Ahoy!-avast!-belayer* and soothslayer, is mine and thine Archfiend.

We who have chosen not to swallow the poison that dissolves pipe dreams with lab-coated, smartsmock exegeses, methinks, are blest with keener instincts. We know nothing is truly knowable. Only the gullible seek antiphons in headpills dispensed by questionable *-tists* of *Science!* ~ the modern apothecary. Why wallow in the muck of knowledge?!! Veritably, the hex of *Science!* is vexatious to the Spirit.

Science!, a false god, is a serpent entwining 'round our everyday lives, enwrapping our very well-beings.

It slithers into our homes without a fear of being *snake!* detected, clubbed to Quietus.

Its kiss is merely the hiss of power-draining devices.

Woebeit, once bitten, forever smitten.

Lo, even a bantling in the bassinet harks the rattle.

The embrace of *Science!* ~ vermin of vipers ~ is the stranglehold wringing all so dashwheel eyewater dry, more coldhearted, dejected.

Who has not detected the slippery silver-tongued devil's guise?

Do not the forklashings of *its* shortcomings ~ *its* lies ~ acerb on the rooftop of our discontentment?

Do you not pang for the simpler hungers we are famished for in our overindulgent times?

The fangs sluice their juices.

Yea, as we whine, we whimpering bluenoses, blubbering dangerously close to the outlets we let into our crave-dwellings, the electrifying, snaky encoilings of the viper-monster further trespass upon our Tree.

Sour-apples, we.

A basketcase of them we have become.

Science!, the Savage, rampages unchecked; we are the junglevines.

Who can claim the Beast is tame?

Unleashed, thy pet atomizes.

Whilst the *-tists* of *Science!* babble about the black holes they sit upon, others of us cope with more believable mysteries. In the swirling dervishes of waltzing thru our daily ados ~ sped up no doubt by the bogus top spinners ~ do we not, also, slow dance away our precious moments in closet meditations? What is reality except an ad interim inner skin of borrowed cerebration ~ the celebration of self thoughts ~ we shed 'tween the memory of fond yesters and the daydreams of bon morrows?

If Life is Reality, then *whatever* we believe in is real-life.

Yet, in actuality, we change, molting as we go. Peeled away realities are our resumés. 'Tis an inner stripping we all do ~ and should do ~ without a blush of shame or a teartrack of sorrow.

Only the walking dead ~ zombies entranced in the nether world of the perpetual present ~ are hoodwinked by their own voodoo cultivated treadmill. Why snuff out the stuff of dreamlands? Surely, the circ of workaday dreamless sleepwalking is ne'er fulfilling nor everlasting.

Those of us who muse on the textures and tincts of cloudfluff ~ thru the tinted panes of hirise office hulls, via the recessed windows of effaceable blackwalled-in classrooms, per the arrow-loop slits or *meurtrières* in the masonry of donjons, by diamond-lozenge eyeviews of hallway skylights or in the windshields of our everchanging minds ~ *we* know there are other forms of floating islands: airlands. Airlands are simply isles afloat in the ocean of ether.

Naturally, not all cloudstuff can contain the weight of an airland within vaporous wisps of flimsy cumulus fibers. Not even a gilt-lined thunderclapper leaming perfectly arched double rainbows in full spectrum hues is a sure sign of the underside of a passing airland. Mostly overcasting above our heads are the gloomy clouds of our own self-doubts.

Frivolous to ponder upon, goldrimmed spectacles of nimbus puff rolling thunderly aloft are rare stuff ~ with or without shades of skepsis or an omen duo beaming forth lucky-mirth.

For what it is worth, reader aviso: rainbows and airlands are both real and hard to grasp.

Try as one can, who has ever been fortunate enough to be caught 'neath the arcsy prisms of a rainbridge's span? To bathe in the flow of the waterbow of an overfall doesn't count! E'en so, to bask in the glow of a sunbow, rarefied as it is, rarely signifies a true airland hovering by. Why so? Airlands are rare. Sky mirages and tricks-on-the-iris ~ even once in awhile blue moons ~ are much more commonplace.

Who inherited the wormy earth, bequeathing to me all this authoritative *wizdom* on kingdoms in the sky? No one, I know of, in persona. Let me jus' say, an inordinate amount of my latter lifetime has been spent on such stratospheric queries as the whereabouts and whatabouts of a very rare wonder of the nature of things: a cloudland in our mists. Granted, I have never seen an airland. *Lee* ~ as in to lie ~ I shan't. I know one exists. 'Tis no sham.

Just how rare are airlands? Airlands are certainly rarer than isles boating on the open sea ~ which I *have* seen. Unanchored sealands are firmly rarer than their frigid counterparts ~ the floating cubes of sweet water that lose their rigidity to delicate whims of deliquesce, even in a tepid salty tub. Beehive any archives or buzz-by many libraries: sparse is the info on most floaty things. *Real* airlands ~ those that do exist in the natural realm of things ~ are few in number. 'Tis my best guesstimation.

In factuality, airlands are not only scarce, these cloudlands are also the most wind-blownt of all lugged objects.

A baby spider, oft no better off at eggcrack than an orphan ~ and always of a broken or unspoken of ma-begnawed-pa lineage anyoway ~ can climb the nearest or highest flower to beget a better beginning.

By catching a passing waft of easy air, the spid can hang-glide on a homespun thread of silkweb and go on a breezy ride into the next backyard, even as far away as a juxtaposing county.

Thereby, the wind-blownt, octad-leggy little runagate can settle down, open up shop, rent-n-tax free, and promptly prey on newfound neighbors.

The locals, taken unawares of the crafty lil bugger's pedigree, intendments, appetite, learn all too soon, all too late, a grim moral.

Spiders, the archetype of shopkeepers, are simply out to slurpstraw the visceral juices of the yokels, leaving 'em as sere as the bonedry dune-buggy tracklands of the Great Southwest Outback.

Arachnids, allwheres, are not insects.

Likewise, not all spidery flyblowns are eight-legged: biped, bimanous two-faced bugs are more wind-blownt than spids and oft bicorned.

Spores of certain weald mushrooms, kith and cuz to wilder inedible fungi ~ identifiable only under the bottle-bottom magnifying glass of a semi-reliable mycologist ~ are said, by some, to be quite adaptable to being wind-blownt by the caprices of airhead whimsy.

Doff off to the duff, methinks.

One has to be daft to assume the only living room in a forest is for trees.

Is a spore the seminium or the ovulum??

Is it a seed? Or is it even the *semlum* of an offspring??

Could it not be a detachable and reattachable part of an overall, already living thing?

It beseems, a whiff of draft to a Mycota fairy ring means more to the growth of megaorganisms living underground, than all the pine needles and nuts strewn upon the forest floor.

Evergreens, surefootsy rooted, reach for sun glow, but are they the overlords of Sylphdom?

Or is the realm ruled by Underlords?

Boarish to mention, the sniffsnoutsnuff of foraging riflers trying to root out silvanian life simply for the inflated economics of piggish gastronomiques: shame on those who buy such Tubers as truffles!!

A forest is more farfetching than latticework of arbor branches, timber clumps, logs, stumps of woody stems.

'Tis wind-blownt, far-reaching, frangible.

The seeds of weeds, every farmer, gardener, boneyard caretaker and lawn manicurist knows, are as wind-blownt as anything can be, almost. Compared to an airland, these puny upstarts ~ spinwebbers, fungus colossus, whatever ~ are but a sneeze.

If airlands weren't propped up and borne by the turbulence of lofty currents, the cloudlands simply would not be islands in the air. Rocky, boulderous masses are big falling rocks ~ BFRs for short. Big rocks falling from the sky are something else altogether. Alarmingly dangerous and unpredictable, BFRs shouldn't be confused with the likes of an airland. Airlands are, more or less, of the noninjurious quarry.

Unless, by mischance you happenstance to live upon an airland. As with any terra ~ firma or airy and otherwise ~ cliffhanging hazards do occur in unlikely loci. Let's face it, a slip of a ladder and *it just doesn't matter...*

Off-colour, on another focus, there's also a worst place scenario: to have the good case of bad luck of batblindly flying into an aviational skerry. Scary and airy mishaps do happen. As sure as there are BFRs. 'Tis little use to fret or sweat. Skyway catastrophe is not jus' an anyoday occurrence. Alas, it is one of the dice rolls in the poker face win-some-lose-some biz of insurance Schemes & Scams. Ante up, gents and ma'ams?

Fornia is just such an airy and scary place ~ 'tis a wandering, mistical airland. It is also a locus for wonders, chosen long ago. How long ago, you might wonder? Hmmm ~ the precise moment in time isn't exactly frozen in amber. Let's jus' say, Fornia has been lugged around for a very long time.

No calligrapher am I. Nor does this cloistered layfra ~ myopic in sight and eyesore to see ~ rheumatized by dank drafts which rust the hinge-bones of my mortal crust ~ envisage a typographer's imprint to be pressed upon the scriven manuscriptic cacography you the reader now hold.

Nor does this humble translator of rare texts, plagued by so many aged illths ~ all of which *Science!* has failed to find medicaments for my carnal predicaments ~ cherish the prospect of relinquishing The Book.

Ah, The Book, the only relish of my chilly, silvering, crow's feet sprawling years.

Nay, this unknown monk, occulted away atop a cliff rock hermitage of one, expects not hermeneutists to review this lifework ~ now done.

To possess a book is to behold the magic of the imagination held within its skiver, its case cover, its skin. A book is a living thing, given a life of its own.

What is life ~ even a *complete* life ~ but a series of unfinished projects?

What is a book ~ a completed book, from hands on to handmedown ~ if not a form of life? Inked words on paper ~ 'tis penblood ~ a two dimensional medium. Encased within its 3rd dimensional vehicle, its skin, penblood lives on in a time machine called *Book*.

Completion is a child. Sort of.

Creation is cremation. Of sorts.

To give life, one must burn up part of one's ownself. Sometimes, one must burn out all of one's self.

Long after the air-blasts of foghorn trumpets faded from my nerve-deaf eardrums ~ a bo'sun whistle no longer my piper's calling ~ my book of hours now are marked with another chime of bells ~ and toll this tale now to be told.

From matins to complin, this tale has never been told before. 'Tis cloudy if it will ever be retold.

Why is it being quoth now?

It is not.

It is written.

It was meant to be read ~ even outloud.

Verily, it is based upon the shaky grounds of hearsay and heresy.

If damnation is to be my crucifixion: sobeit.

Damn *Science!* for my sins.

A book once befell upon my tabletop. Albeit, it fell into my hands in a roundabout way. 'Twas a tome of rare vint ~ a wooden codex, cryptic in contents, caliginous in origin.

Decades spant I, hunchbacking laboriously o'er the confounding work till I was near spent. Ne'er were my slouch-arching, masseuse-abstained shoulders relieved by analgesic gels, the anodyne ointments, the anesthetic creams of *Science!* ~ the shyster, the snake-oil drummer. Pathetic became my stooped posture as my freeze-dried frame shrunk into my bonebag. A score of annums and *more* spant I ~ excruciating backpain-in-the-arse years ~ whetting my wits on a Rosetta stone to crystal the mist of the Great Wooden Tome: The Book.

Heaven forbid, The Book first came to ground in the late '60s. 'Twas found in the backwash, lunar-cratered Mojave, nearabouts where some half-forgotten-n-half-neglected *Injun* reservation treads lightly next to an unnamed Army artillery and bombing range.

Hallelujah, The Book was not destroyed by those who tried to zero in on it, near-missing, or the authorities who did not decipher it ~ missing by a mile ~ or the scholastic academia nuts to whom The Book was turned over, who could not decode the text. Mistaking the tome, and taking it out of context, *they* branded it a 'pranksterish wooden bookbomb' hoax!!!

Fain as the disciples of *Science!* were to unlock the secrets held within the mysterious wooden opus, their brainstorming *hocus-pocus-open-sesame!* thinktanks ran blank as soon as their grants were due up for expiry.

Their unpublished and denounced sequiturs are barely worth repudiation.

For awhile, The Book was mulled and glossed over by several learned Paters of Theology ~ those well versed in the speculative studies of *Palimpsestic papyri* ~ who deemed The Book not worth another *divinitive* look.

Known to be a man of the world, of words, a definitive patron of Pagan *et* Profane lettrure, a former seafarer and in dire need of firewood ~ The Book was brought to me. Dropped on my desk along with a cord of kindling and a big box of 'strike anywhere' kitchen matches by a burly brute, methinks was mute ~ whist was his mode. A terse attached note read:

Do it yourself heretic kit:
add sectary

Thankful for the unsolicited donation, I delved into the merciful, elephant-oversize contribution to my bookshelf editions with conviction.

Yea, as I grew tusktoothed and my gum-meat receded ~ relieving bowels sanctioning no relief to my intestinal grievings ~ came the day I bowled over all the linguistic impediments the Ph-deedledumb dissertationists stumbled on!

'Twas *their* fault! *They* knew not what *they* were doing.

Pigeon-hawkers, money-changers in a house of prayer ~ even pewed bingo parlors ~ altho contemptible practitionings are sufferable sins. Criminals are *-tists* of *Science!* and scriptural scrollmongers undertaking the task of unraveling the works of a contemporary shortform artist! As sure as the ziggurat dedicated to Marduk on the plain of Shinar was pure Babel, the ivorytoothsaying watchtowers of another sunbaked era know naught about the Divine inspiration of dreams, nor of the interpretation of poetry.

Is it not amazing how the glowth of a waning waxen grows most lambent as the wick flickers from candle lux to a lit puddle of tallow slush?

So, too, as I melted with the gravity of age, pulled downward by the all-equalizing force, I saw the light-life of The Book in all its lucent glory. *It* came to me on the wingspan of an angelic dream.

They surmised The Book to be the hijinx of some dopehead, pot-smuggling, pinko, antiwar hippie-type!

They said The Book was too recently 'done' to be of ancient or medieval origin, too primitively compiled to be of normal modern binds and bounds, and, too earthlike in form to be of extraterrestrial composition.

They were so close, chose to be so wrong!

They claimed The Book was tossed from an airplane ~ in an air corridor 'known' as a flight path for dope runners ~ because it left a big crater in a bombpockmarked wasteland devoid of craigs, hills, other natural lofty platforms.

They stated it was dropped on the military post as a peacenik protest because, like now, it was a time of civil unrest, and an unpopular war was waged and raged in our living rooms. Popular wars are hard to come by, no doubt about it, because *they* usually begin in streets.

They pointed out the type of wood used to create the 'leafs' of The Book came from an unknown species of tree ~ footnoting that the jungles of the postconquistadors were brimful of dopers, Cheist guerrillas and unclassified vegetation. (Less brimful now, than then.)

They insisted The Book was 'written' in no earthly language, past, present, future and/or otherwise. *They* moot their own points.

They know nothing about The Book.

They never transcribed The Book.

They have forgotten how to interpret dreams.

They are not inspired by poets.

They are like lost soles from a shoe ~ going nowhere.

They would believe a weaver of words could sacrifice an entire lifework, a hundred pound wooden tome, as a protest! 'Tis not dissent! It isn't penance; it makes no sense: bibliocide?!!

Now, as I shiver in the donjon of my dim-lit cell, robbed of warmth by thieving chills even my hooded cloak and robe can not fend off ~ gimped by stiffbent kneecaps, crutches for a crux ~ some may think me a grumbling, embittered old grump. Nay, *nay*, not I. Not as I clutch The Book ~ freshly translated.

Naturally, not every word of The Book could be anglicized verbatim. What is safe to say, is that I have cracked the essence of the original 'text' ~ the poetesques of a nebulous tongue.

The 'writing' of The Book is composed of woodburned-on markings on thin plank pages. Some of the woodburnings are painted in with a strange sort of pigmentation, undefinable of source. Some of the plank pages are blank and the blank 'leafs' leave me to ask myself: was The Book completed? Perhaps not, until now.

The bizarre inscriptions of the handuscript appear to be similar to a melange of cuneiform, runic, pictograph and Sanskrit ~ which it is most certainly not ~ and arabic numerals with a smattering of obvious punctuation marks, a few of which are liken to exclamation points, erotemes, ampersands and arrows. These queer symbols must indeed be what they seem to be. Also, distinguishable diacritical signs, such as alif, wāw and yā show up, as in the Qur'ān. I admit, in editing the text, I omitted many, most, of the confusing signs & symbols.

What does all, or any, of this signify? For the benefaction and *benefiction* of those who are a bit stumped: my storyline. What *Science!*, the slithering fork-tongued slurpent, hash-slings out as 'facts' can be done and redone by any-many methods.

I believe the author of The Book to be either a poet or a prophet. Perhaps neither. Who can say for sure? Why dither on the ether of that? Truly, words alone can not express the exact impressions felt in the wet-cell grey matter of thought batteries. The poet, or scribe, of the epistles, now translated, is certainly an enigma ~ if not a mystic, then a mystique. *His* ~ for he *is* of the masculine gender ~ writing style, as far as I can decipher, is well versed in bardic scripture. His syntax, a dearth of diction unlike the logorrhea of the picapicaticatica type writers, is, however licentious in any lexicon. Word-burners, methinks, are like that.

Where does this author hail from? Selfsame place The Book fell from. 'Twasn't an airplane. 'Twas a passing airland. In this particular case, the cloudland of Fornia. How can I be so sure? 'Fornia' was the third inscription I was able to make-out. 'ob' or 'av' was the second, and I, quite rightly, take it to mean *of*. The first 'word' of The Book was either a name or an epithet ~ of which the man has many. 'Calif' < *caliph, khalif* or *caliphe*, *He* chose.

Many parts of The Book were obscure in its original form. It lacked the necessary narration and background material. Moreover, altho the handuscript was (is) several hundred plank pages long, after translation, the work wasn't 'booklength'. Fret not. What is a translator if not a good editor?

   A *Versionist!!!*

There are those who will be my detractors.

   They will say I translated nothing.

   They will say I only updated my own book, begun decades ago.

   They could never give me credit for narrating things which escape their clasp ~ questions to answers beyond their grasp.

   They will say I made up stories.

   Some of them will go as far as to say I, *I* dropped the wooden tome out in the desert!!!

   What do *they* know?

Now, I know the warmth of the 10ber summer ~ yea the icy horn bloweth.

   Where's the original wooden tome?

   Xed somewhere in a safe haven.

   To my detractors: *beshrew you all!*

      Behold, he cometh with clouds...

      Retold, he cameth with a cloudland...

Fornia must be older than our continents ~ formed when the mighty winds swept o'er the surface of the waters, yet unlit by the separation called day. By the time dry land appeared on the Sphere, the airland in the Atmos must have already been blest with The 21 Wonders...

Fornia probably flies above our heads at an altitude of jus' about a few thousand feet over our highest mountain peaks. The airland's cruising speed is unknowable, even changeable. The unchartable course of the cloudland must be a zigzagging whirl-of-a-wind...

2
THE
THREE
GODS

Fornia is an island
In the air,
An airland clouded
With castles and hassles
Everywhere.
In an Atmos of fear,
Amid evil and civil despair,
The 21 Wonders
Of The Three Gods
Are enshrouded there.

Fictionary

<u>Stick People</u> < us, short-form
<u>Stick People With Eyeplugs In Their Noggins</u> <
> us, l o n g - f o r m
<u>Sphere</u> < earth; a dirt ball
<u>Atmos</u> < airy region high above Sphere
<u>Index Prohibitorius</u> < list of best selling books
<u>Amaranth</u> < 1. an imaginary purple flower, fade-proof 2. a real purple basil on Fornia; also, the colour of the Royal Emblem of Fornia
<u>Myriotheism</u> < misbelief in many gods
<u>Mystagogy</u> < 'art' of explaining the Unexplainable (!?!)
<u>Ex nihilo nihil fit</u> < nothing + nothing = (?)
<u>The Great Black Umpthing</u> < almost everything that is not anything else
<u>Cigarette turd</u> < 1. the almost intact ash of a lit cigarette tip that lands anywhere but in an ashtray, especially long ashes looking like something out of a kitty litterbox 2. the stick person responsible for such a loathsome act
<u>Benthos</u> < bottom depth, as in an ocean ~ or something

Long before the land dragons took to the wing on the surface below, there was the airland of Fornia gadding about above. Long before stick people with eyeplugs in their noggins stuck out on the surface and struck out after drumstix on the sands, seas and skies of their Sphere, Fornians were living aloft in the Atmos.

Long after the stick people with eyeplugs in their noggins overpopulated their Sphere, they half-heartedly took to Space. Like misguided and spoiled children, the surface dwellers like to leave many spacecraft toys strewn about *their* solar system. Being an argonauty lot, the surface dwellers don't care if roller-skates or skateboards are left in the driveways of real Space and Time flybyers.

The Fornians, on the other hand, are not by nature anything more than a haughty lot. In their Atmos, what's Upst or Downth isn't even taken seriously yet. 'Tisn't *their* fault. Just as an airland is hidden from a surface dweller's view, almost everything is nebulous from a cloudlander's standpoint. 'Tis always cloudy and forever windy. Arrested social development, so-called, isn't exactly a genetic curse. It is a blessing bestowed on the more fortunate.

Even before the pushy stick people on the Sphere took half-heartedly to Space, they bent their stiff rubbernecks upwards. Why? To pond on perplexing probs which neednot concern 'em. Like who begat whom, which is ancient history. Or the permanence of the firmament, which is older than prehistory, the Index Prohibitorius and In The Beginning... Even prenatal care.

Fornians mind-wander on more delicate motifs ~ like the *whatabouts* of The Rainbow Bird or the *whereabouts* of an amaranth herbary.

Sphere chuckers, for some unknown rhyme, grabble with all kinds of *whatnots&saywhats?!* More featherbrained, perchance, than the ideas brainstormed on Fornia.

One is the Great Question of myriotheism ~ which is, of course, unknowable.

Another is the jigsaw puzzle of mystagogy ~ which is truly a mystery.

Neither of (†) those concepts are pursued as religiously as the Fever of Cortez, or whoever. → 'Tis the fervent passion to obtain the status of Deity of Glitt'y, a social disease. Verily, it is an illth curable only by the medicament of unworked-for Gold, Silver, Gems and the lesser gods of the underworld ~ or the Pale Horse: a cureall.

Still other lifequests on the Sphere are spant in quiet meditation: the Reverence of Silence. A true and noble concept; especially for mountain stick people.

The strangest of all surface dwelling conceits is the Pursuit of Unhappiness ~ or *Science!* in the short-form.

(†) Knowhowhounds of this kennel try, *try*, to steeplechase over the hurdles of espying the Expanse of Space from a spinning, sunbathed, cloud-enshrouded dirt ball somewhere off-centre from the Middle of Nowhere!

Furtherless, *they* look thru optics and know not the illusions!

Who is not hoodwinked by the eye, when the *magic* of light, shadow and mirror mirage?

Surface dwelling stick people with their feet more firmly planted in terra cognito envision a House of Heaven ~ and await confirmation.

All conceptual sects on the Sphere have their own dogmatic rites and customs. All groups like to dogtailchase t'others around. None are right-on nor left out.

Space *and* Heaven are there.

As are The Three Gods.

Few feeble thoughts have ever been chiseled out of the thick blockheads of stick people and more apropos to be carved in stone than these:

Ex nihilo nihil fit.

Excluding perchance, this witticism of criticism:

A schoolyard bully and a childwithchild
are both prepared for adulthood
and should be graduated
ahead of class.
Not after.

Never is longer than forever. The former has no beginning, zilch of a midriff bulge, nothing of a tailpiece.

Never was there a time when there was nothing.

There is, and was, The Universe.

The Universe has always been godded by The Three Gods.

The Three Gods know things. The Trinity of Infinity knew long before anything was created in The Universe, that there was something to create with. That something isn't much. Never was. It is enough. 'Tis dust.

Collectively, The Three Gods got up the gall to gather up a lot of the stuff. Call it *cosmic* dust if you must.

The Three Gods thrashed the dust three times, like chaff, and the stuff formed into a cloud. As the dust cloud settled down, it condensed into a wiggly mush. The Gods meshed the mush into a mash. Out of the mess swam a mass: The Great Black Umpthing!

Henceforth and ever since, The Great Black Umpthing swims the almost empty Empyrean Sea, sees all, says nil.

The Great Black Umpthing is the oldest of all mortal creatures. 'Tis also the wisest of allkind and by far the widest of all critters in Creation ~ *why?*

Size is a dimension. The big backside of The Great Black Umpthing blots out most of what can be seen by anything with eyeplugs in its noggin ~ no matter the vantage point anywhere in the visible macrocosm.

Moreover, its rumphide is the greatest source of invisible **X**-ray radiation ~ a tried-and-true carcinogen to stick people, like the ones prone to flicking lil cigarette turds on tabletops.

Following the wonderous creation of The Great Black Umpthing, an apocalyptic III-way schism twixt The Three Gods *almost* nixed the next-up stage of evolution. In The Beginning *almost* did not happen...

To corkcap the spouts of ungodslike poutings, The Three Gods spittooned their spiels on the kismet of their first created Thing in the then much smaller cuspidor of Space *and* Heaven.

The exact words of The Three Gods, then as now, go unheard. To ad-lib, or rather *ad-scrib,* an envisaged rendering of the roundtable rap session would be a very *Versionist* thing to do.

Uno God: "Let us create another Umthing.
Downsize the amplitude, a wee bit.
Change the colour, perhaps.
Maybe a few frills would be nifty."
Duo God: "Add a few *thrills* ~ indeed!
Why start another project?!!
Let us *finish* this one off, first!!!
From dust *to* dust ~ is a must, trust in me!!!!
Thy revelation is waste created Thing!!!!!
Resurrection is reusing the dust!!!!!!"
Tri God: "ăåâãàáäąwwň..."

Let the record show a half-yawl yawn and shoulder shrug were the responses.

The Three Gods ~ *Life, Death, & Indifference* ~ thusly set the tones of the three godslike tunes.

By chewing the straw and gnawing the jaw, The Three Gods finally came to terms ~ but in no tempo of time that can be danced upon in the eardrums of stick people with auricles protruding from their noggins.

The Great Black Umpthing could live.

It would be the only Umpthing.

It should live only as long as ne'er was heard one umpth out of its um.

"Go now in one piece!" The Three Gods bade without farewell.

'Twasn't necessary. How afar can The Great Black Umpthing go?

Next, The Three Gods made another, smaller discovery. If littler amounts of dust were used ~ as compared to the great quantity kneaded to form The Great Black Umpthing ~ and the stuff was swirled around a bit, the dust clouds condensed into dust balls. These dust balls are not unlike the dustbunnies that seem to come out of the Middle of Nowhere, as from under beds and other infrequently swept areas. 'Cept, the dust balls of The Three Gods are much bigger.

Eventually, something very unlikely, even iffy, happened. The Three Gods inadvertently said something like 'fiatflux' simultaneously and a dust ball compressed so tightly as to ignite from pure friction!

The strange & fascinating restriction of elbow room ~ which produced torch balls out of dust balls ~ pleased The Three Gods. The Trinity of Infinity called this revolutionary wonder of the nature of things 'macaroni' ~ or doodlenoodle in godsly colloquialism.

The torch balls are denominated by a very long name. Only The Great Black Umpthing has lived long enough to hear the godsly name all the way thru, and only once. We know they're called 'stars' if far away and plural, and sun or Sol, up close in the singular. Or *Disc* on Fornia ~ where stars aren't seen, or known.

Oft, on impulse sprees, The Three Gods have said the abracadabra word to glowth dust balls into torch balls. Vast branches of the cosmic tannenbaum became gaslit up with garlands of the twinklie lil lights. By accident, The Three Gods determined that *any* godsly word spoken at the same time would *ta-da!* a star! Creation by accident is undoubtedly a wonder.

Stars, made up of the simplest of things, pleased The Three Gods immensely. Why? Elementary. Stars are simple machines, self-contained and require no costly upkeep. Nor do they have to be replaced all too often. And they make more complicated things ~ like dirt balls, which are smaller. The Three Gods dubbed each lil dirt ball with an individual agnomen ~ or 'planets' for a generic surname.

Planets do not light up like torch balls unless compressed very tightly by the 'doodlenoodle' effect. Then they glow only very briefly before turning into a fog of reflective dust ~ a wisp of almost nothingness.

Verily, the only thing The Three Gods enjoy about the dirt balls are the way the bulbs are smartly spaced and hung around their mother(s) star(s). Alas, not all decorations are pleasing to The Gods.

Some planets steal other planets. No biggie. Larceny is not a cosmic crime. Nothing is ever really lost or found in The Universe. Everything is reusable and re-recycled, *ad infinitum...*

Other planets create their own dust clouds. Some of these planetary dust clouds condense down, in part and particles, to form useless and ornamental things ~ like rings, even *moons* or 'satellites' in the nonsense. *Moons* glow in the dark. Such satellites aren't real lights. And are not supposed to be. They're really only big, or lil, mirrorstones ~ apparatus for optical illusionists to gawk upon.

Moons are not only unnecessary, they're also quite noggin-boggling time-pieces.

The Three Gods did, and still do, grumble a little about the vanity of dirt balls. Vainglory, nonetheless, is a minor sin when compared to Hamartia Major ~ a constellation in the starry Necklace of Night.

Hamartia Major ~ or *Sin Big* ~ 'twas where *it* first happened...

Some planetary clouds condensed down into wetter stuff than nebular dust. Water droplets rained down forming puddles on the dirt balls. From the ooze of the mud puddles came forth a la minute life forms. This mystery of the nature of things, at first, bedeviled The Three Gods ~ tho not very much. Lil things are very hard to see anyoway.

Ultimately, The Three Gods came to be disappointed with the little a la minute life forms. Why? The darn things began to combine into much more confounding things, which are very hard of listening.

Over a starcloudy period of time, imperceivable with a lunar or without a lunatic calendar, wet stuff clouds rained afar and avast from the original connect-a-dot twinklie string of Hamartia Major.

Thusly, a la minute life forms became as common as the cold thruout Space *and* Heaven.

The Three Gods agree: where there are wet clouds there is water. Where there is water, there are a la minute life forms. Where there are a la minute life forms, sooner or later, will come the stick people with eyeplugs in their noggins.

To a God, 'stick people' are simply stuck together alaminutelifeforms.

Nebular dust and nubilous wet stuff also make stranger, more *shroudy* things than stick people, stars, planets and their useless rings and *moons*, and all the commonplace things in between.

There are more outlandish things in Space *and* Heaven.

Stars-that-are-not-stars-at-all are there, tho not truly rare.

Airlands, out there, too, are doubtlessly the strangest and rarest of all cloudy formations.

Collectively, torch balls, dust balls, dirt balls, dust and wet clouds, free floating specks of dust, parts of The Great Black Umpthing's e'er present rump, stars-that-are-not-stars-at-all, e'en airlands, make up almost noticeable little clumps. The Three Gods call these dusty globs something like 'muckyways' in the past tense, or 'galaxies' in the present sense. Why? 'Tis unknown, unknowable. To the Trinity of Infinity, galaxies are the size of snow-flakes.

To The Great Black Umpthing, galaxies are beacons of small thought-waves on a pabulum web, excluding the background static of minor disturbances caused by primitive clans of stick people using lethal electromagnetic wavelengths, microwaves, other light&dark bands not yet banned by their Elders. *Lethal* not to Umpthing, but to the users: mostly losers with cordless ring-a-dingies stuck to their noggin sideflaps.

Collectively, galaxies appear as strands of interwoven silken threads embroidering some intricate pattern befitting a cosmosaic piece of Byzantine masterwork ~ or something.

Tsk tsk to the –*tists* who wish to get such an overall looksee at The Universe! One would first have to move most of Umpthing out of the way, a feat not even Atlas could meet.

The Three Gods, being pleased with the motif of the catholic-cosmic-cloth soon returned to the godsly game of Godsupsoneship, a pastime similar to Oneupsoneship, an ungodsly game played in temporal, temporary courts.

The Great Black Umpthing, more appeased by the spectacle of the strung out colossal fabric of galactic threads and small thoughtwaves, simply concentrates on the repast, not fasting the time away. And ne'er has been heard one umpth out of its um.

Silence ~ the most noble of all sounds ~ is usually inaudible to the eardrum. As has been read, The Great Black Umpthing has not been heard. That is, out loud.

Shhhhhhhhhhhsss, whist, *hushup*!!!

'Tis a murmur of a rumor: a certain oeuvre-deaf airlander finds the tone of an umpth to be quite a-pleasing over the tinnitus seashellish windsong hiss of his nerve-wracked tympanum.

Ummm, that story still belongs in the future ~ the afaraway future...

Godsupsoneship, the aforethoughtly mentioned game of The Three Gods, soon manifested into the materialization of a grand project: The 21 Wonders. The 21 Wonders are wonders for a simple reason: the rules of the nature of things ~ mysterious as they are ~ are N/A to these creations.

Each of The Three Gods created 7 Wonders apiece. Why 7? 'Tis a dice roll in the chancy ifdom of the unknowable.

The Three Gods turned The 21 Wonders into an art project of celestial magnitude; except on a much miniaturized scale. At length ~ but not within any sands of stick people time-frame, encased in glass and flipflopped o'er sanddown to sandup ~ The 21 Wonders were completed.

As with any *voila!* works-of-arts, godsly chef-d'oeuvre, or otherwise, a problem arose: what to do with the Masterpieces?

Another catastrophic Ⅲ-way schism tween The Three Gods *almost* Xed out The Universe!

Soon it became apparent The Universe wasn't big enough for the godsly egos of Three Gods! The godsly swellings of the Trinity of Infinity, not unlike head trips, soon expanded Space jus' like a beachball being inflated.

Only The Great Black Umpthing didn't seem to shrink ~ much.

Only by yet another roundtable chitchat could The Three Gods avert the comingon chaos.

The Universe was coming undone.
Galaxies began eating galaxies.
Novas, once rare, became commonplace.
Supernovae, heretofore benign, went berserk!
The Great Black Umpthing squirmed a bit as it swam in the emptying, *already* almost empty Empyrean Sea.
Some stick people became unstuck, returning into a la minute life forms.
Many a la minute life forms dissipated into wet clouds, which in turn, became dust clouds.
The Universe was becoming a dust bowl, jus' like before In The Beginning...
Countless dust creations went *poof!* before The Three Gods acknowledged any godsly goof-ups.

Life wanted to share The 21 Wonders with all of creation ~ a noble endowment indeed.
Death damned, demanded and DEMONstrated in words and ways that can not be emulated except by the throes of *Death!!!*
& Indifference cleared phlegm from the oft unused godsly throat organ and took centre-stage in the three-ring performance. Ignoring the honorariums *Life* was portending to laurel upon the cosmos, disregarding the wreaths of wrath *Death* was ring tossing 'round Kingdom Come, Tri God tried to unwind the airbag tirades with a bit of lassitude, a touch of wit.

& Indifference looked around as if about to address a throng of lent-ears in an odeum and leaned 'gainst an imaginary podium:
"What is the thrust of a lightning spear
without a drumroll of thunder?
Why piece together the shards of a bust
once the idolatry is put asunder?
Whence a waxing without a wane?
After the apexing, thence the bane.
Who can take back that which
has already been given?
Why scratch what does not itch?
Why drive when one can be driven?
To jingle a chain can be a jinx.
To plunder even 1 Wonder
Would be a blunder, methinks.
Who's going to help us clean up the mess?
Why all the fuss? 'Tis such a stress!"

Neither *Life* nor *Death* had heard such a gift of gab or such poetaster chitterchatter out of the godsly windpipe of Tri God before... Both Gods were floored!

Even The Great Black Umpthing, was taken aback ~ a little.

Albeit, no living, dead or resurrected stick person with auricles in their noggin has ever truly overheard the words of a God ~ being hard of listening by the nature of things. Everyone has overheard gossip. That's gospel.

The Three Gods haggled for a fortmillennium, and more, then concurred as The Great Black Umpthing tried to eavesdrop on every word.

"The 21 Wonders are too wonderful to wind up in a midden..."

"Too fabulous to be a 'fruit' forbidden..."

"No doubt, The Wonders should be hidden..."

"What about..."

Mute went the utterings and mutterings of The Three Gods, even to the pth of The Great Black Umpthing.

Hmmm ~ thought Umpthing diving deep to the benthos of its vast, expansive network of wet matter intellections. Wishywashy thoughts leap-frogged off lilypads splashing murky reflections.

The Great Black Umpthing thinks alot.

Thinking too much is a dunderhead pursuit.

Pondering on The 21 Wonders hit Umpthing like a thunderhead! What *cloudland* had survived the stormswells and undertows of the Great Expansion?

Fornia! 'Tis a wind-blownt, uncharted airland far removed from any known ports-of-call. Its tenants ~ a sept or sect of stick people or ants ~ 'tis hard to tell from such a great distance, not that it matters, know naught of The Three Gods or The Universe, and nothing of The 21 Wonders! Fornia! What a perfect obscure dot!!

Ymmm ~ thought Umpthing.

3
ANGELS OF THE AIRT

Harps do herald:
A Heavenly Messenger
Takes to the wing.
Hymns are caroled:
O what tidings
Dost thou angel bring?
Psalms be spoken.
Frankincense
Burns at the altar...
A wing is broken!
Canst thou angel f
$$a_l$$
$$l$$
From Grace by falter?!

Fictionairy

Anteportico < an outerporch where colonnade stand guard; usually the frontispiece of one's manse
Dunno < don't know (?)
Cockahoop < cock-talk
Airt < 1. the wind 2. the direction in which the wind bloweth 3. an angelic passion for blowing around dust
Pulchritudinous < same as uglisome from the inners-side
Dustbesomdust < same as sweepbroomsweep
Ng < as in The Great Black Umpthi*ng*, a part of The Universe
Bizzbugbuzzbeelzebul < Fornian bumblebird-talk
Nawnawna nawna < origin unknown; meaning unclear; (!?!) perhaps a *taboo* word
Th < from *Th*e Great Black Umpthing; a piece of The Universe about as far away from the ng as one can get
Brunosia < art of a brown-noser
Ab ovo usque ad mala < 'from egg to apple', for those who have ne'er dined at a Patricius banquet before watching the lions devour the Christians in the circus; or 'from beginning to end'

No spirally stairwell vails from the anteportico of Space *and* Heaven to the backdoor doormat of anywheres. No dangling rope nor wheelchair slope aids the +athletic inclined or the −plegiac confined in groping with ascent or descent in the cosmic sense. The celestial ladder is rungless, unscalable.

How does one aspire to the godsly gates? Ya don't. Can't get there from here.

Mountains, tho spiritual places, are not high enough. Not nearly. Nor are airlands ~ lofty places ~ or airplanes aloft.

An engine with boosters is as bedecked as *Science!*, the tinkertoyer, can outfit for a bon voyage thru Shallow Space, the destroyer of stick people, their playthings. Regardless of all the cockadoodledoo cockahoop, *Science!*, the henpecked rooster, is closer to cracking the earthegg with its rockets, than laying one on a Heavenly object.

No terraced stepping stones, hopscotch stars pave the flight of height from Upst to Downth.

Empyrean Sea architecture is dizzyingly infeasible. Besides, in the strict economy of The Universe, frugality is the proverb.

Even to erect a single file footbridge ~ a major engineering feat and sole sore ~ is cost prohibitive when vast stretches of dusty almost nothingness are involved and infrequent is the intended traffic.

The Three Gods, having completed The 21 Wonders, already allknowing where to stash the trove, nextly had to contend with the task of *mode of transport*.

Where to ship the treasures to, is one thing. *How* to schlep them there is quite another.

Even for Umpthing the moving job was a ?!?

The Three Gods knew, to ask The Great Black Umpthing to lug The 21 Wonders would be a dumb, ungodslike thing to do. 'Twould be like coaxing a slug to *get along now, lil doggy, heeyah!, gettyupgo!* 'Twasn't that The Umpthing is a little slowpokey ugly, slimy bug ~ even to a God. 'Twas the fact that The Great Black Umpthing is so big it would take forever for it to swim there. Never would be the time for it to backstroke back. Moreover, to ask Umpthing would require an umpth. Only *Death* beckoned with such a coldhearted, hotheaded reckoning, *& Indifference,* as usual, abstained.

For The Three Gods to do it, 'twould be very ungodsly. There is a line twixt&tween working with hands and manual labour. 'Tis called Art.

Of course, *not!* The Three Gods did *not* use hands to create The 21 Wonders! Pinky fingery things are ungodslike.

The Trinity of Infinity did blow some dust around a bit. Blowing 'round the stuff created with dust isn't jus' work, it is another stick-mark in the dirt. It is called Airt.

The Three Gods refused to crossover unto or into this ungodsly compass!

So, The Three Gods ~ in factuality, *one* God ~ created something else: Angels of the Airt.

Death was off on some holocaust.

& Indifference was around, but didn't contribute a zephyr of anyothing.

Angels of the Airt were an easy enough godsly thing for *Life* to cook up. Jot down the little recipe, if you'd like:

Firstly, *Uno God* got together a fair amount of the finest, floury dust.

Secondly, speckles of a few freckles, ummm, a hump-hair or two ~ both ingredients plucked from the rind of The Great Black Umpthing ~ were thrown in. As were seven *moon*spoons of star-baked glitt'y stuff.

Thirdly and weirdly, *Life* blew in jus' a pinch of *Uno God*stuff.

Nextly, a smidgen of salt and a ton of honey were added, as well as two turtle-doves, seven Welkin pigeons, eleven handlebars, a pair of kid gloves, countless compass cards, astrolabes, sextants, orreries, eyes of silver needles and golden pinheads, Jupiter-size diamonds, a dash of crystals, a dozen bedchamber gowns, halo crowns, zithering lap-harp strings, and some zest of zip, zap and zing.

Lastly, and least of all, *Life* blew in a gusty breathwind of Space *and* Heaven ether.

After a time ~ longer than it takes to break bread ~ a diosmosis took place. All the above ingredients settled down into △ triangle-shaped eggs.

After a short incubation period, hatchlings pecked out ~ stranger than birds!

'Tis an easy enough recette don't you think?

First off, as the Angels of the Airt took to the wing ~ blowing 'round dust as if it were inbred ~ *Life* called upon *The Children* to blow The 21 Wonders o'er to the prescribed spot. A breeze of a mission, done with no more ado than was due all the to-do.

Next up, *Uno God* vociferated for the Angels to tidy up The Universe ~ blow lots of dust around. Afteritall, The Universe was somewhat a messy place after the Great Expansion.

Withal, The Three Gods grew tired of blowing 'round the dust Themselves ~ and from Their godsly toils, They did thus take withdrawal.

Leisure became the pleasure of *Tri God.*

Death never takes a holiday but does take holocausts for pleasure; lives at leisure. Great Extinctions tickle *Duo God.* As do sickles.

Life enjoys holidays, vacations, weak-ends, an eterne night's rest, and whatever else ~ it is anyone's guess.

The Angels, to accomplish their onuses ~ or as they like to call it among themselves, their 'anuses' ~ are specially equipped with nothing more especial than a *pair* of things. (Shame on *those* who think: overtheshoulderboulderholders or jockeystrapfrontflaps!! Angels are purely asexual beings!!!) The *wings* of an Angel are the true workhorse of Space *and* Heaven.

Now, the Angels of the Airt are not a *perfect* lot. Most are good. Some are a lil bit naughty. A few are downright *uuuughly!!!*

Being a goody-goody Angel is the pompom cheer heard most oft in myth. In sooth, only the most obstreperous Angels ~ pulchritudinous *or* uglisome colloquy-stoppers and head-turners ~ are sent off on special assignments. Why so? Space *and* Heaven is Absolute Upst, the Apex of Allwheres, the Peak of Perfection. To go, and be, anywhere else is *like* heading in the direction of Downth. Who'd want to be a downcasted Angel?

Many of the Angels like to sing or whistle whilst they work. It hides the irk. Alas, the niche of an Angel of the Airt is not to hum or strum, as some might assume. 'Tis to flapbeat their wings. Blow some dust around.

Dustbesomdust!
Sweepbroomsweep!
Keep the dust moving!
A mustbemustbemustbemust!

Some may shirk, others may smirk, but to a God ~ preferring the Symphony of Silence ~ nothing is worse than thorn or thistle than to have to listen to an underling sing or whistle!

Angels caught birdsonging on the wing ~ or snitched on by snickering goody-goody pompom squealers ~ are downgraded. And chalked up on the Demeritus List.

Keela-la is not a goody-goody pompom angel, does not have a stick of tattletailfeather in plumage, isn't e'en very naughty, and is as far from *uuughly!* as a Fornian is haughty.

What is Keela-la? Jus' at the tiptop of the Demeritus List. Top Angel for chalking up a humstrumming-humdinger of a Demeritus score! Otherwise, Keela-la is an A-OK Angel.

Maybe Keela-la is a bit too much talkietoo for an Angel of the Airt. Then again, Angels aren't a perfect lot.

Perhaps, Keela-la is a bit too tall for an Angel, afteritall ~ heighth can be a handicap. Makes you peer out of the crowd. No doubt about it, most of the Angels are weighty. Keela-la is mighty heighty!

A God and an atheist have only one thing in common: neither entity recognizes t'other.

'Tisn't *always* the fault of a stick person, or even a whole stick people.

Sometimes, The Three Gods hide the obvious in plain sight. And even under the best of situations, most godsly things are camouflaged from stick people with eyeplugs in their noggins ~ like how to live. Unlike a bird or furry-tail or wormy bug or seed-bud, which are all, more or less, endowed with knowing how to lead their lives, stick people must learn the ways of the nature of things. Mostly by being taught.

Far away on Fornia, a man is listening to an inner calling ~ an a-pleasing *uuuuuuuumpthhhh* which fills up his malleus and incus, oval and round windows, cochlea and all the other little semicircular and vestibular marvels which make up the gut-works of an inner-ear. *It* only happens when he is in deep concentration.

He knows not from whence *it* comes. He doesn't know why. *It* jus' comes-on.

He thinks, or rather senses, something is plugging into his thought-waves; tho, *'plugging into'* is a foreign concept to a Fornian.

Oft on impulse, or compulsion, he conjures up vivid, exactingly precise images in his mind's eye. On another world, *photographic memory* is the term. On Fornia ~ where history is written not with the sharpest recollection but with the cloudiest of effaceable reminiscences ~ he is known as a bardic storyteller.

Bardic storytellers, the ones plagued by good memories without the device of mnemonics ~ or *memoria technica* in the dead-language of the momento mori sect ~ are seldom the concern of Gods. This is because lesser, more down to the ground underlords usually do them in, or under, before they stick out too much. Underlords are jealous zealots.

Unless some synesthesia, as tween Umpthing and *some thing,* is going on.

An *uuuuuuuumpthhh* can cause a lot of irk...

Fortunately for Keela-la, not too many special assignments pop upst in Space *and* Heaven. Why? Angelic messenger service calls are not the hallmarks of good godsliness. Plus, since the Great Expansion, before the Angels of the Airt were even created, little fuss has been made in the Upstmostsphere by the Trinity of Infinity. And less pother has been made about the goings-on in Shallow Space.

Up until...

Keela-la is blowing some dust into a cloud, nigh the ng of The Great Black Umpthing, when it starts flipflapping its ing!!!

"Bizzbugbuzzbeelzebul!" humbugs Keela-la like a Fornian bumblebird as the Angel wingspans up and upstward in a swirly-hurry.

Hovering nearby, another Angel of the goody-goody pompom eggcrack ilk, blows dust into dust-ring letters: *"Nawnawna nawna!!"* ~ or something in taunt or tease. Heedless to say, the twit is needless.

The Three Gods already take notice of the commotion and looksee 'round The Universe to see what the fuss is all about.

"Ah," *Death* blurts out "see there ~ there's a Fornian 'bout to go o'er the Ledge-Edge! How creative a suicide! O how juicy, too."

"What's that?" asks *Life*, a bit puzzled.

"A book, a big wooden book," says *Tri God.*

The inging thrashsplash of The Great Black Umpthing is a big cosmic convulsion. Star clouds kick up into whorling glitter drifts, not unlike a shaken up **X**mas snow-glass-water-globe. The ing of Umpthing, far, far beyond the Empyrean horize from all stick people with eyeplugs in their noggins on the Th to gaze upon, warbles. 'Tis only the curvature of The Universe that saves the spinning marble Sphere of earth, and the flying-carpet airland of Fornia in the upper Atmos from utter destruction.

Needless to say, High Court is held in Space *and* Heaven. To include all the legalese soapbox testimonial tonguewaggings in the transcription of the Tribunal would be the waste of a rain forest and most of the Pacific Northwest ~ already rain forest wasted, more than less.

Hark the charges ~ and the handmedown thru an angelic dream ~ verdicts, pleas, please....

The Great Black Umpthing, charged with an indeterminable number of illegal attempts to try and communicate, via nerve-deaf vibes with a certain oeuvre-deaf Fornian stick person, for the sole purpose of ascertaining the whereabouts of The 21 Wonders...

Plea: not an umpth

Verdicts: insufficient tangible evidence; dust to dust; & dismissed.

The Great Black Umpthing, accused of inging its ing and causing the greatest disturbance of and in The Universe since the Great Expansion *because* some certain oeuvre-deaf airlander was about to fall over the Ledge-Edge, perhaps e'en taking a word-burned inscribed wooden book filled with descriptions of The 21 Wonders with the lowly miserable selfsame...

Plea: not an umpth

Verdicts: blameworthy; shameless; & abstain.

Summary: "Go now in one piece!"

Mattmarkluke&john, or Pall to some, an Angel of the Airt, twit-class, misdemeanor charge of violating the Symphony of Silence, no prior chalks ups on the Demeritus List...

Plea: "'Twasn't *my* fault! Keela-la said a *bad* taboo word!" Note: the defendant kowtows before the Thronely Trio, cowering in whimperish *brunosia.* "MiGods, show lenity, Your Graces, ne'er 'gan shall, will... shan't happen again."

Verdicts: guilty as sin; sinfully giddy; & *Twerp!*

Sentence: clean up the ing sector of The Universe, forevermore!!!

Summary: *"Nawnawna nawna!"*

Keela-la, an Angel of the Airt, heighty-class, arraigned with the felonious transgression of mimicking the mating call of a certain airlandic fairylike creature of one of the Lowliest Orders in the nature of things, *and,* the minor offence of violating the Symphony of Silence, with *how* many priors on the Demeritus List ?!?

Defendant: "More than are in the cipher 'Ø', miGods."

Life: "You're tall for an Angel."

Death: "Do you have a wish I can help you with?"

& Indifference: "Pleas, please."

Defendant: "i, i am guilty, guilty & guilty. i think i used up all my excuses, long ago."

Verdicts: guilty; guilty; & guilty.

Sentence: volunteer for special assignment ~ all the way downth to Fornia!

Summary: "Keela-la this shall be your Last Judgement! Fail at this chore, kiss off your wings evermore ~ ta ta!"

Fly down, down past the Th of The Black Black Umpthing.

Below, beneath the spillage of the sunken Space village Hornacorn.

Adown, below 'tween the Rings of the Onyx Onion.

Bedown and beyond the Shifts of Red, White & Blueth.

Spiral adizzingly downward thru the Wermin Orifice #9.

Flap down your wingtips near the dimwitted star ~ devoid of solar mate; white with yellow hairlight.

Check your zodiac chart for these Shallow Space ☆ signs:

♈, ♉, ♊, ♋, ♌, ♍, ♎, ♏, ♐, ♑, ♒ & ♓.

Flit down until you begin a gliding descent.

Beware of the roller-skates and skateboards strewn around by the childish stick people in this Shallow Space area as you glide by.

Bypass the dirty slushballs arack.

Be wary of the slimy Ⅷ-ball ~ it's as black as a Space ♠ can be.

55

Follow downth The Balloons of Gases ~ they are buoy masses to guide you in safely to harbor.

Turn down towards the blasted pieces-of-bait of Dirt Ball, Xed.

Skirt the Red Rusted Rock.

Prepare yourself for a sudden stop.

Head for Marble-Sphere-Swirled-by-Dead-Moon: Fornia floats above this globe always at High Noon.

Special Instructions: do not break seal until at this downth level of Shallow Space.

<u>*Catch falling book from falling what's-it-name and return with same. Do not ~ repeat ~ DO NOT!!! ~ return with the stick person ~ The Book. Repeat: RETURN WITH THE BOOK!!!*</u>

The Angel, following instructions *ab ova usque ad mala*, successfully flybys the toyish junk strewn about Shallow Space. Oooopps!

An orangey looking cable satellite in orbit o'er the Sphere, mistaken for a fig leaf, might as well have been a banana peel:

$W_{o_o o_o o}{}^{a}a_a$ $W h^{o}{}_{o}{}_{o} o p p^{s!}{}_{!}$ ~ $W^{h}{}_{a}a^{a}t h_{eeee}{}^{e}{}_{ee}{}^{e}$ ~~♭♯!?!♂⇔♀!!!~~ ~ was the first true sign from Space *and* Heaven in a very, very long time.

4
BEFORE THE FALL

Time, the arrow twanged
'Tis a shaft ne'er reclaimed
~ & this
Need not be langued...
Only by lore's hourglass
O'erturned to lad & lass
Canst thou returneth to
& grasp ~
A time greener of grass...

Fictionairy

<u>Nebbia</u> < the Fornian cloud-cover, usually about the tincture of the Martian sky on a dust stormy day (orig. (?) Dantesque vernacular)

<u>Emeraude</u> < an aude spelling of emerald, the green colour

<u>Flutterby</u> < mostly lepidopteran fairylike gad-abouts like colourflies and their duller mothy kith bugs-on-the-whimsy-wing

<u>Disc</u> < The sun as seen on Fornia thru the nebbia; looks something akin to an upsidedown fruit, or something.

✟ For referencia, consult solar phenomena in any physics -*tists'* handbook dealing with the reflection & refraction of light on ice crystals, etc. Better yet, looksee for yourself on clear wintry nights. The sky is a spectacular wonder ~ full of magical events, free, & your's is the best seat in the Heavenly House.

<u>Disc dots</u> < 2nd cousins to sundogs

Fornia's cloud-cover umbrella ~ or nebbia ~ is as beauteous a sky as e'er arced o'er the airland. The day is an awe of fluffy shades of blush & rouge. Umbras of varying shapes flit with strobe bursts of shade softened shine ~ flirting & waltzing 'cross emeraude hills & tarragon dales. Flutterbys dart about, alight upon windflowers of a palette-sweep of tincts in a dance that delights the scented vista with fairylike choreography.

The vertex Disc ~ always a delectable eyeful ~ dishes out its soothing apricot-fuzz-orange-blossomy glowth with the usual green garnish: an inverted, leafy-looking stem.

As if on guard duty, two roundel shields ~ or Disc dots, off-true rainbow in hue ~ are positioned on antipode flanks of the Master whom these imitators attempt to mirrorstone.

Nacred arcs, halos & other sacred sidekicks the Disc, at times, keeps 'round, aren't present for skywatch as is oft times the sight.

The hunchbacking hillslopes, silvery-bearded with raggedy wisps of fog-whiskers are dotted with florets of broccoleaf bushes & other burseed bramble. Some are strewn with clumps of bloodberries, a common birdfeed.

The giantry of leafy vegetables in view, the gnarled soakwoodia trees ~ dwarfed only by the mammoth-trunked Sequestoia arbors hidden in The Impassable Cloudmounds ~ scatter & cluster 'round the slopes as if by choice. Some of the wooden statuary stand in stout solitaire postures, outcasts to their a-stemmed breed, defiant in stance 'gainst the ceaseless winds. Most of the proud overgreens seem content to congregate in family gatherings, branching out together in the nestlings near the mossy-rocky runnels dribbling towards the spongebogs. The runnels always funnel down the wrinkly creases of the weatherfaced, humpbacking hillsides.

The felt-green carpet of grapplegrass, lawn-covering most of the airlandscape, seems to purr as unseen hands caress this pelt of living fur in crosswind waves & convulsive swirls. The low-bred verde ~ every blade a shaft of life, an entity unto itself ~ bows & curtsies to the everchanging whimsies of the gusty blores of invisible overlords & miladies.

Merely finding breathing space in the alfresco must be a chore to those growing in such overabundance. The groundcover of a hillside is not a velvet cushion of vegetational snugness.

And yet, this animate plant life layer of root-&-stalk is living proof of the still sensitive outerskin of an undead world.

Most worlds ne'er get past stillbirth; ejected stone-cold dirt balls, abortive aberrations of whatmighthavebeens.

Many worlds are retarded at birth or die in unnamed infancy.

Some worlds make it thru to adolescence; a few make it past that trying period.

Still fewer grow to adulthood.

Rare, *nay, Blest!*, is the world that lasts till full abloomed maturity.

Such is the natality rate of living worlds.

The fate of an alive world depends upon the fertility of low-bred greenth & their grains ~ the munch, the mow, the mulch of the organic things which live on the skin of the world.

The grassroots of Fornia are a hearty breed. They need to be. Wan is not the lot in life of namby-pambies. Those punies who are bred on the nutrients of spring water, the miracles of feces and guano intermixed with common dirt furrowed by the burrows of limbless tillers are the stuff of bread: the staff of life for most of the 'higher up' commonalty. The staple that feeds the bulk of life is weeds.

The beauties of nature are as free as a sigh.

The bounty of a lifework oft leads to a neigh.

Whence comes the whinny of an unseen horse.

"Heeeyaaah!" is overhead, not understood. It comes from a camouflage of foliage, a hill-hump away.

A condor, circling aloft on random buzzard patrol, swoops into figure-eights & hawkeyes at the disturbance and the trespassers.

As the hooves of a heavily laden steed gallop away out of earshot, an aperched owl hoots a toot or two at the sleepwreckers.

A faroff soakwoodia tree emits the caw of a crow.

A man emerges from behind his concealment: a bloodberry bush. Cautiously taking a looksee, making sure he is out of harm's arms, he hand-cups an ear to try & hear better.

5
BICCH
OF THE
BIBLIOWERMIN

The first outbreak
Of the plague
Are vermiculations
So very vague...
It feasted and fasted
Till it outlasted
Almost every illustrated page.
The outburst of outrage
Over every worm-eaten
Handuscript ~
'Tis written off as
Apocalypt...

Fictionairy

Bicch < a dice throw of a word; meaning unclear, but aliken to many expletives

Bibliowermin < book illustration & illumination eating worms

Vermiculations < pertaining to worms & their squirmy ways (?)

Featherdowl < fowl feather stuffed

Frufra < something fancysmancy & unnecessary

Initials < Overly capitalized words (?)

Uncials < style of handuscript word-burning in vogue before punctuation was in flower

Wedknot < 1. a bow tied in wedlock 2. a knot not unlike one used for shoestrings

Wall Tax < the keystone of all cityslickers' burden, first enacted when the first wall was erected

Drossel < an old name for a practitioner of an even older profession or avocation

Moly < 1. an imaginary flower 2. a common windflower on Fornia 3. a type of garlic worshipped by pyramid-building cults

Shewn is sitting in her bookshelved show-off room, showing her midgrownup son ~ a Male Child Brat, or MCB in the vernacular ~ a slab of a map placed heftily on her lap. As with all airlandic cartography, the Bicch Of The Bibliowermin have already gotten at it. Only place names remain on the worm-eaten plaque.

"Mom" moans the MCB in a baritone of a voice more prone to hail from a grownup man than a midgrownup son, "why are we looking at a wormy ole map?"

"Shhhhhhhhhhhsss, whist, *hushup!!!* I'm trying to connect the dots with my thoughts."

"What dots, mom?"

"Imaginary ones, hon."

"Bizzbugbuzzbeelzebul!" the antsy lad becries as he squirms and pouts on the haystuffed divan, slouching over a featherdowl bolster.

"Sheathe thy tongue or sharpen thy wit and quit fidgeting!"

"Mom, what good is a map, anyoway? And *that* one doesn't even have a cartouche! Not even a windflower!! It's missing all of the imaginary monsters and all the splendid fancies of make-believe!!! It doesn't have *any* illustrations!!!! You can't even dreamland on it!!!!"

"Oh sure you can, son," says she " imagine our world shaped like a, an, ummm, sort of like a giant dragonbug in flight and we are all riding on its back. Besides, I don't want the missing drawings and decorations to come back ~ look at all my books!!! After the frufra motifs and illuminations are eaten off, what's left but some artsy, oversized initials, a few uncials and a pinch of symbols!?! I want more words!"

"Mom, maps aren't suppose to have *more!*"

"Hon, I was referring to words on books."

"Oh," says he, looking 'round the room at the tomes, tomes, tomes.

A dearth of words can be a terrible blight to some ~ even in a semiliterate society. Shewn's cottage is strewn with wooden tomes. Some from the best and many from the least read literati on Fornia. All her walls have built-in shelves for the elves of literature to dwell upon. Even the headboard of her featherdowl bed is said to be bookended with candle-holder lamps custom-made of brass and glass soasto mirrorstone more glowth just for the unheard of purpose of reading in the slumber-chamber. Her kitchen cupboards hoard volumes of books instead of jamspreads, branbreads. And to light up her firebrick stove, she first has to move out the most cherished titles of her booky trove. Even her indoor water closet is a lil librarium of written material to choose and read from. Shown is no writer; Shewn is a reader! At least, 'twas the case before the plague.

"Mom, on what part of the back of the dragonbug do we live on?"

"Depending on your point of view, son, either nearabouts the tailend of the bugger or nearer to the head. Definitely not in the middle."

"I prefer heads to middles and tails."

"Mom, what does *terra incognito* mean?"

"Hon, it's jus' the cartographers' excuse for not leaving their mapshops and hopping about to prove the whatabouts of the whereabouts of geographica."

"You mean they scibe about what they don't know about?"

"Yep. Son, mapmakers, experts and a lot of writers are like that. Wood wasters they are."

"How can you tell a good writer from a wood waster, mom?"

"Good writers ne'er quoth quotes except from ghosts. Good writers are supposed to be word-burning scribbling originals ~ not woodburner scribes of another's original. The proof is in 'the read' and 'the write' ~ not the renditions. Besides, a good writer knows it is best neverever to consult any mappy thing. The realm of a good writer ~ a wordsmith ~ is supposed to be unchartable. 'Tis where they want to go ~ to the unmappable ends of their word-burning beginnings. Also, expertise is a hindrance to all good writers. Good writers are born out of frustration ~ altho' not necessarily out of wedknot ~ forged in the nittygritty smitty of experimentation. Good writers make lousy students and laureate professors..."

"Mom, you're footloose at the mouthing!!! You read *too* much! Maybe, it's good the bugs have eaten up your books!"

MCB ~ thinks Shewn ~ you have no idea how far I'd go to get my hands on some reading material untouchable by the Bicch Of The Bibliowermin. She cerebrates these thoughts, unknowing how far she will *have* to go to find some booky thing worth 'the read.'

The MCB sits up and takes a closer looksee at the map upon his mom's lap. "Mom, even without a worm-eaten map, isn't the general topography of our world somewhat *shroudy?*"

"Not really, dear," she points out "do you see here ~ that's De Vow Lay. That's where we are at."

"What's that?"

"That's *El Lay!* You know that. Don't be so clueless! We live outside and over-the-hill from The Walled In Town so we don't have to pay the Wall Tax, silly. I've told you that before."

"Mom, why'd you and dad decide to untie the wedknot?"

"What!?!" Shewn blurts out to the abrupt change in thought direction. She wishes she could sometimes see inside her son's noggin. Rethinking that thought, she then shakes her head, nodding: *naw!*

"Not what, *why?*"

"Son, your father and I are good friends and the best way for us to stay that way is to be not too close and unwedknotted."

"Mom, what are all these ugly names?"

As sure as the Bicch Of The Bibliowermin ate all the mappy drawings off Shewn's carte, the following ugly names are lifted right off the selfsame graph:

        Zooman-Ville
        Two Hatch A Pee
        Gee-No!
        Front Terror!
        Vax Ax A Ville
    Cull A Knee At Sandless O'Pisshole
        Coronera
        Foulsum
        Stand-In Quicksand
        Stole-A-Dad
        Tracelessly
        Jammed In A Stone
        Corkacan
        Anvil Knoll
        Nork Womb-Fact
    Done Again At Rock Mountain
    Shuck-A-Walla At Blight
        Was So!
        Mule Creak
        Pale-A-Can, Baby!
        De-land-No!

And others too numerous and ugly to name.

"Hon, those are dungeons."

"Why do we have so many dungeons? Fornia seems to have more dungeons than Fornians!"

"Son, you will understand more about that when you are older." Shewn says these words even tho she *is* older and doesn't understand. For certain, she is planning the outline of a trip in her brain ~ and wants to avoid running head-on into one of those places.

"Mom," queries the MCB looking at the map and noticing letters larger than most of the other place names, "why is it called 'The' Oblong Valley?"

"Son," replies Shewn, "'The Oblong Valley' is called so 'cause of its so-called shape. 'Cept it's actually shaped more like the umbra of a giant peanut ~ if you could get the monstrous goober to stand up and cast a shadow."

"Why is it in bigger letters than most of the other names on this rotten ole map?"

"That's because it's one of the most distinct features of Fornia, hon, altho not one of the most distinctive." She makes this up knowing that The Oblong Valley is another good place to avoid ~ more so than any and every dungeon.

"Mom, what's in The Oblong Valley?"

"Not much. The Quean, son, the Quean," she says, grimacing, reshifting her body weight.

"Mom, what's the matter, don't you like the *'Queen'* of The Oblong Valley?"

71

"It's not *that* drossel or the Bicch Of The Bibliowermin that's eating my guts out at this moment ~ it's this map! Help me lift it off my lap, it's hefty!!"

With a lot of help from her not so little son, Shewn manages to flipflop the wooden slab unto the mudbrick floor with a *thudplopthud.*

"Wheeeeyuuwowwee," says she, relieved.

The MCB muses at the thought of learning a new bad word as he notices the new hole in the mudbrick floor ~ caused by the fall of the worm-eaten map.

Shewn gets up from the haystuffed couch and brushes off the stray straw needling onto her skirt-bottom. She says to the MCB "Now get packed up, we have to get going soon. I want us to leave in about an hour."

Glancing 'round her bookshelved show-off room she wonders how long she's going to have to be gone from her MCB, her cottage, her windflower garden. A trip oft takes longer to undertake when one knows not where one is really going. What she does know is that she has already stopped at every bookshop in El Lay and all The Walled In Town's environs. And every book she has come across has already been subject to the loss of gloss, the scourge of the Bicch Of The Biliowermin.

"Damn the Bicch!" she shouts to herself.

Shewn ponders on the route of her journe, her first out into The Inferior of Fornia. De Citi ~ the *next* and only other Walled In Town in the Kingdom ~ eight days away by hoof or heel, along The Windy Way, is the only other place that isn't a dungeon or a dunghole.

A wormhole burrows into her brain: perhaps De Citi and its outskirts are pretty ~ not ugly and dirty like El Lay and its rambling outburgs. Anyoway, thinks she, with a pleasant outlook, unlike El Lay, De Citi has no trail leading into or out of The Oblong Valley. 'Tis a big plus, in itself. The Oblong Valley ~ the source of so much trouble these days...

The MCB returns to the show-off room all packed up like *he* is going on an adventure of unknown duration, but is hesitant to get his foot out the door. "Mom, are you taking The Grapevine to The Oblong Valley and then The Beeline thru there?"

"No, honey," responds his mom, "I can't get to where I'm going from there. I'm going to try and take The Windy Way."

"Mom, I ain't never seen a Queen ~ do you think I ever will?"

"A *quean!?!*" Shewn gulps, then regurgitates "I don't think a lack of *queans* will ever be a problem ~ jus' take 'em and leave 'em."

"Mom, how long will I stay with Grandma?"

"Until I return. Let's go."

Off the two stroll to Granny's shanty, a short trip down The Rutty Way.

Once they had to stop and leapfrog hopjump over a pothole so full of potty water, the MCB wanted to name it. He thought ~ I'll call it 'Holey Moly With A Lot Of Water', or something. He didn't tell his mom this thought. He knew better. No one in this part of Fornia calls water anything ~ except 'El Lay Water'.

Naturally, it does not rain on Fornia ~ Fornia is an airland. It rains *under* a cloudland and always. The floating isle in the air also rains down Fornianwermin ~ or what the ignorant stick people living underneath the passing airland call 'earthworms' in their ignorance. It does not matter. Neither Shewn nor the MCB know they live *on* an airland. To them, Fornia is *the* world. *And* even if they did know that it rained worms and water drops beneath their feet, they couldn't have cared less. They would know it was a matter which neednot concern them.

The MCB wonders where water comes from, and so makes-up a make-believe scenario in the backstage of his fertile imagination: *water falls ups' from the ground, then dripples downt' to the spongebogs, there the trees squick their toes and ups' it squirts from the water logs!*

Shewn eyes the MCB from askance, hmmms ~ what is he ever thinking so much about?

The MCB spouts up "Mom, where does water come from?"

Shewn simply tells the truth "Hon, all water nearabouts El Lay comes from someplace else. Somewhere afaraway, beyond The Oblong Valley ~ over The Impassable Cloudmounds, yonder still, further than the farthest hill. It comes from the Pale Of The Shadowland. 'Tis where the Bonedry Clan hardscrabbles."

"Don't the people there need *their* water?"

Shewn ponders on this wonder before replying off the cuff. Hmmm ~ Our Lady Lord Mayor, The Great Dame of Greater El Lay, *she can't remember the name of her-wickedness* ~ says that the people where the wet stuff comes from don't use water, need water, want water. So, it's only the charitable thing for El Lay to do, to catlap-up what the non-needers don't lack. "I think they are dirt farmers, son."

"What then, do they drink there, mom?"

"They don't drink, hon. They eat bonedrydirt to quench their thirst."

"Mom, are you going to go there?"

"No, my son, a place without water is not a growing greenth spot ~ it's jus' a dirtbowl. I'm going where there's trees and word-burners. I don't think I'd find either there; too deserted."

"I doubt they breathe ether there, either."

Whilst the pair pingpong talk as they walk, Shewn paddles up her thinking creek a wee bit faster. Hmmm ~ could it be, to juice up El Lay we squeeze-dry other folks so we can gulp? She tries to imagine a world without water ~ 'twould be as dull and drear as watching time thru a sandglass...

"Mom, why are you walking so fast? Wait up ~ what's an *hour?*"

"An hour is an artificial lapse of time that can not be measured except under glass, nor comprehended unless by the movement of some predetermined amount of something, confined in something else. And *we* are walking this fast 'cuz I'm in a hurry ~ now scurry up to me!" Shewn makes these things up jus' as she runs out of breath and the two arrive at Granny's shanty. She's glad. She doesn't want to be mind wandering on the thought path she's been straying on.

As Shewn drops off the MCB she grabs some garbs from Granny's wardrobe and dashes into the garderobe. When she reappears, the MCB beseems to think his eyes are erring.

She bids adieu to her precious two and sets off on her journey.

Standing in Granny's doorway, watching his mother hobble away, the MCB asks "Grandma, is my mom an old woman, now?"

"No, my dear, your ma's a smart cookie."

6
THE FEATHERWEIGHT AND THE RAVEN

Kaw kaw kaaaawhaha!
'Tis the cackle of the
Vile raven!
Shoo away you mavin
Of carrion!
No mazard
Pickbones for buzzard
Bait await
You here!
'Tis graven on a ledger:
Kaw kaw kaaaawhaha!!!

Fictionairy

<u>Mavin</u> < a connoisseur, of sorts; also *maven*
<u>Mazard</u> < thy noggin's skull
<u>Bugaboo</u> < ragamuffin*ish* (?)
<u>Inferior</u> < any part of Fornia not Walled In ~ nor nearabouts a Walled In Town; the outback
<u>He-Man</u> < singular form of *he-men*, a term from The Brawns Age
<u>Sheeban</u> < a sorceress
<u>Patois</u> < real & used language as compared to proper & fanciful notions of speech considered to be the acceptable standard; the latter requiring a stiff upperlip & other artificial inflections
<u>Ornis</u> < 1. avifauna 2. all the ornery birds within a certain *-is*
<u>Malocchio</u> < 'the evil eye'
<u>Matranees</u> < plural of servant girl
<u>Laughodil</u> < a silly, lil flower ~ origin unknown
<u>Featherweight</u> < a poet or poetess on Fornia
<u>Penblood</u> < an inky pigment used to colour in woodburned word-burnings
<u>Carnivours</u> < what the canine teeth of a carnivore can do
<u>Nve</u> < horsetalk

The quarry of the unseen horseback huntsman doffs his floppy hat to his newfound friend & safe haven ~ the bloodberry bush ~ in mock gesture of gratitude. Who is this scarecrow of a man? Why is he being rabbitchased? Is he a craven coward? Eyeing his surroundings in quiet lassitude, the bugaboo of a man beseems wary, as if, even here in the Inferior of Fornia there can be found no solitude. Eliding the evince of *a shoo!* a raven hedgehops o'er his hobnoggin & alights upon the bloodberry bush jus' as he's dusting off his bramblethorned tush.

Kaw kaw kowtow kowtow! crows the raven as if talking to the ragamuffin man it is gawking at.

"I bow not to He-Man or Sheeban ~ nor do I kowtow to crows! Buzz off, yon blackrook, afore I take a rock to you!!" so says the man as if talking in the patois of the ornis.

Kaaawhahahahahahahaaaaaaaaawwh!!! caws the raven flapping its wings in kneeslapping guffaw. Bloodberries & twigs bail from the bush.

The man gives the taunting bird a malocchio glance & the raven responds with a monocular daw eyebeam.

Silence & stillness reign in the harmony of a single moment.

Even the ceaseless wind seems to holdback a breath.

The man blinks, dropping the piercing gaze of his evil eye.

The raven gives a wink & pretends to tend to the task of plummage.

The man turns his attention to the terrain...

He's wind-blownt in posture, bonebag in stature ~ disheveled & dust-strewn in dress. Grubby is his overall mein.

On first glance, he may seem a rogue worth avoidance. Mean might seem his demeanor to some. Albeit, to the bird, it appears he is mostly of a noninjurious vein.

Neither nearabouts the waning of the sallow-yellowy-ghost-blueth tongue of his life-flame, nor newly ablazing in the callow candlewax of adamhood, the man's tallow wick burns evenly, his age is anywheres in between.

His face is well-weatherworn. Crow's feet tailfan from his squinting orbs ~ the facial tracks of a lifequest spent searching, perhaps. Worrylines burrow upon his brow.

Beneath a bird-beak proboscis grows a black caterpillar of a moustache ~ with jus' a wisp of silver in the sable. Protruding from a V shaped chin, the man sprouts a gruff clump of billygoat tuff.

His britches are baggy, bulging as if multi-pocketed. Confessional: 'tis hard to tell thru all the layers of road dust.

Yet, where *is* the road?

An overcoat, or duster of sorts, hangs down longer than is in vogue. The original colour of this outer garment is of undeterminable tinge. Perchance, it is a cape on closer look ~ 'tis clasped at the chestbox, draped over the shoulders. No armloops dangle.

A checkerboard vest is buttoned across his chest & the cuff of a blouse shows thru at the collar. 'Round his wind-apple a kerchief is tied, rainbow hued.

He lugs no baggage. Not a shoulder bag. Not even a quiver, much less a purse.

Kaw kaw kaaaw! Tailfeather in the straw! mimickbirds the raven.

Another might be taken aback by this sudden blurt of a blackbird. Not so, this one. He takes his eyes off the countryside & surveys the ground.

The raven swoops from the bloodberry bush & scoops up a very large feather near the base of a solitaire soakwoodia tree. It lands near the man's feet, dropping its beakful & hops about the ground pecking up fallen bloodberries.

Picking up the plume the man hmmms ~ 'tis a tailfeather indeed! Moreover, 'tis a quill pen!! Tsk tsk, it's out of penblood.

"Much obliged," the man says in thanks to the raven as he sticks the stylus into his hat.

Kaaaw! Kaaaw!

"What would a plume pen be doing out here & *you*," he asks turning towards the raven "why are *you* here?"

The raven caws no answer. Instead, the bird winghops up unto his shoulder to roost.

"Yes, I knew a knight once who taught a raven how to jibber like a mimickbird. You're much too plump & too accustomed to talking to strangers to be a wild thing on the wing. Are *you* that selfsame bird?"

The raven replies not.

The man begins to move out, walking with a sense of direction.

"Awe," the man says to the raven after the two have hied half the day away "the dawe is a delight! I hope we reach the road before the rise of night."

Kawhahaaw! Hahahahahahaaw!

Even in the midst of beauty, the stealth&stalk of danger walks. Its tread is lightfooted. E'en in the dance of daylight, for there are those who do not tread the gametrail at night, the orchesis of prey & predator plays the tune: *consume & be consumed...*

Crossing thru a field of windflowers, knee-deep in fairydom, the man pipes up a little jig as he struts along:

>*A poet without a patron*
>*Is as barren as a baroness*
>*Without a son*
>*To bearhug the baron*
>*Or a matron without*
>*A household full of*
>*Matranees-in-apron*
>*To look down upon*
>*In ugh!*

Kaw, kaw Featherweight, kawhahahaaaww!

The raven's roost gives way as the man flops down into the meadow, laughing like a soused madman.

"Hahahooooaahhhoah!" the flowers bellow as the bird takes to the wing in !?!

The raven circles in small loops waiting for the man rolling in the laughodils to come to his senses. As he sits up, the bird flies off out of eyeshot.

Resuming his trek, the man keeps his eyes alert for the raven's return. In his head, he splashes around some swishyswashy idioms ~ mostly idiotic:

> *A poet without patronage*
> *Tisn't any better off*
> *Than a tree without foliage,*
> *A blindman on a pilgrimage,*
> *A professor, ummm ~*
> *Barred from tutelage (?)*
> *A sarge lacking a squad*
> *To equipage (!?!)*
> XXXXXXXXXXXXXXXXXX

Cerebrations closer to the mark hit him ~ what's a featherweight doing out here in the Inferior? No court to jest in, no croft to nest in... What's a poet without penblood? Why spill one's guts out? He shouts:

"I HAEMORRHAGE!!!"

It skims the hymns of the winds & goes unheard, unmeant. Once given ~ nothing can be taken back.

Pangs echo in his bellypot as he trudges on. He thinks of food & comes up empty-minded.

He wonders ~ why is it taking so long to cross this windflower meadow?

The first wisps of dusk rise when he comes upon a fresh footprinted swath in the flowery grasses. His own!!!

Delirium ~ brought on by a myriad of causes, mostly self-denials ~ takes shapes & shades & even figure-eights! The man realizes he's been walking almost in a wedknot.

Dehydration & fasting take their toll ~ the man sits down in his tracks. He plucks a fuzzball laughodil stem & makes a wish before blowing the fairies to the winds.

The daisylion, with spots of windrose plots, lets its pounce springforth unannounced.

The daisylion, the flowery feline whose paws hide thornspiked claws, eats horseflesh.

The daisylion, with canine fangs as sharp as flintstone, carnivours any blood & bone.

The daisylion, ne'er known to moan or groan, will e'en devour the flowers of its own.

Kaw kaw kaaawhaha! caws the raven hedgehopping the top of a daisylion about to pounce! The man draws on an inner reserve of strength & turns to meet the sinewy foe ~ almost invisible & yet only a leapfrog away!

"YAAAAAAAAAAAAAAAAHHHHhh!!" he screams as he lunges to greet his fate & plunges into a thicket of rose petals ~ flushed of cat, but not all claws. "Oooooocheeetah" is heard.

Featherweight! Kaw, kaw, hahahahahahaha! Featherweight in the straw! kaaaw! fades into the distance as the raven flies away to shelter for the night.

Before the man finger-tweezers the thorns from his hide, night rises, hindering his efforts.

In absence of chalice, one can go without drink for a day, fortified or otherwise.

Provender, if not provided, is little more than fasting, a welcome relief to the digestive tract at times.

To live without dreams is premature curtains. Eyeshut comes early & easy to the weary man, the meadow his fragrant bed, a mat of grass his pillow, the veil of nightfog his blanket.

Cricket, cricket, cricket, cricket, cricket...

Once, he thinks he overhears the goodnight kaw of the raven.

Deeper in sleep, he dreams he harks a sound like a 'whiiii' coming neither afar nor anigh. Could it be the nve of a horse?

The dawnfall will hasten in a better day ~ aw yes, better...

Featherweight in the straw! Kaw kaw kaaawhaha! Kaw kaw kaaawhaha! Kaw kaaawhaha...

A laughodil speaks "I think I'm broken."

Another answers in a whisper: "Sssshhhhhs. You'll wake it up & it'll trample us all! Give it your seeds ~ *so your offspring will live!*"

7
SALMON RUSH TO DIE

Eggs do hatch.
Minnows do spawn
& salmon do fly!
Come the season
To breed & die
The fishes do one
Last good deed
& fulfil a basal need·
Tender to the table
A noble feed!

Fictionairy

<u>Mead</u> < meadow in Poet-talk
<u>Piscean</u> < the realm of fishes (?)
<u>Dindin</u> < dinner ~ ruminated & slavered from the thesaurus storehouse of words for same
<u>Natator</u> < from L., what one must become in waters over one's head
<u>Eyries</u> < plural of eyrie or eyry or aerie ~ a birdnest nestled in a high place
<u>Columnest</u> < loftiest (!?!)
<u>Darnes</u> < from *dalle* an extinct word in the jargonnaise of Kitchentalk meaning thick slices of raw, deboned fish not necessarily *steaks* or *filets*
<u>Crudités</u> < foods eaten raw

Dawnfall catches the man in the mead in need of rye. In eyerubbing disbelief he sights a flock of salmon flying o'erhead ~ in low formation ~ descending to splashdown. Ymmm ~ thinks he droolishly. Even an umpth isn't keeping him from the thoughts of lipsmacking lox. Rabidly, he races thru the field of flowers & up a hillslope. He hears the saliva of a stream foaming 'gainst boulders. He knows the fishes are rushing into the spring from which they sprang ~ 'tis a rite done since langsyne ~ & plunging forward, shoulder-to-shoulder, soon to die in droves like good little foot-soldiers.

Cresting the crown of the hill, the man bolts down the obverse slope not pausing to catch his breath nor take a lookover of the unbefore tackled obstacle course. Soakwoodia trees & itchvines entwine the incline. Granite piles & jagged heaps of quartz jut in-&-out of his way. His dexter foot fails his balance & he slides into a slid. Grappling onto tugarope foliage, the weaklier end gives way & with it, him. *Splash!*

He finds himself taking an unscheduled bath, unslated for a masseuse.

On the thrill-ride of their piscean lives, the ascending salmon beat their wings like fins, tail-thrashing uphill 'gainst the flow, the rocks, the sloshing man.

Things can happen in rapids, & in quick succession.

The man whitewaters down the rivulet, half drowning in the froth & fish.

Submerging backside up, emerging head-bobbing, then submersing topsy-turvy, he waterslides past...

Rocks big enough to be dubbed 'Mount'.

A grizzly tarpit mammothon snorting water into its treetrunk snout & spraying it out again ~ almost as if wheezing. Or sneezing.

A watersogged log 'bridge', nearly splintering his noggin.

A grabcrab claiming a deserted isle.

Another grabbling with dindin.

Finally, calmer waters, & deeper, remind the unscaled, gill-less natator he is unskilled in the aquatic art of *how-to* aswim. Luck has its ways ~ he touches bottom & sloshes to the bankside.

Kaw kaw! greets him. His newfound friend of yesterfame has beat him to the feeding grounds of the waterbreeders. The raven aperched upon a rock gawks at the featherweight & haws *Kaw kawhahahahahahahaaw!*

The drenched-to-the-bonebag man, no longer acursed with an unquenchable thirst, says nil. Sitting down next to the crowing raven, he peels away his wet wrappings & slaps 'em on some convenient rocks to dripdry. Hmmm ~ he dazedly thinks: now I know why salmon spend most of their lives in the currents of ether, building eyries in the columnest of trees; rivers are not restful places.

Across the water, a good distance upstream & downwind from the barely hairy biped, a momma ursa is teaching her minors the finer points of clawing salmon.

On espying the sheared lewdness of the baa-ing creature ~ or whatever is coming from the barely audible beast's muzzle, to her 'tis a puzzle ~ she suspends class momentarily.

Especially so, after the naked wader wallops a few floppy fish with a branch & paw pails 'em into the mudmuck.

"Now," says she to her cubs "that ain't no way to go afish'n! Yu'al grows up & beez thata o' way, why'll, I'll 'a eat ya both, I will!"

Her uprightly advice goes to no avail. Recess is recess ~ be it kindergarten or how-to-be-a-better-ursa-school-of-hard-headedness.
Romping in the dustyard, the cubs wrestle a harmless game of 'I'mgonnaripyourfaceoff'...

On the other strand of the run, the man, now decently attired with his cape, scrapes the scales of the catch of the day with a penknife ~ surprisingly not lost in the downwash.

Lacking flintstone & steel & other *know-how-to* methods of striking up a fire, the man contents himself with scrunching the darnes of the salmon as *crudités*, altho he finds the raw fish more digestible taken in smaller bites.

The raven, delighted that the nonflighty thing shares a similar passion for such delicacies, feels honoured that it is presented with the juiciest cuts ~ the heads & guts. Kaaw ~ ponds the raven: *peabrained as I am, what did I do to deserve such desserts?*

The man fills his gullet as another flock of salmon splash into the water & dash upstream.

"'Tis a good place to spend the night," the man comments, not expecting a response.

The silent raven pecks & preens at leisure.

A gill away, water sounds are spoken "Hey! worm-breath who da ya think y'ar' poken?!"

8
THE GRASSY KNOLL

*'Twere seven bloomtimes
& a half past
Since thy path
Hast crossed here last.
Tho the span of time
Is not so vast,
Long shadows cast
Auld memories
From yon grassy knoll...
Sire, do kneel
Before thy mound:
Good glaive
'Neath the blady grave.*

Fictionairy

Bloomtimes < plural of a season on Fornia
Glaive < a sword
Cressets < old-fashion indoor & outside lighting devices
Groined Ceiling < frufra curved edges formed by the intersection of arches as in the overlays of some cathedral*ish* structures
Colée < the ceremonial buffet, or blow, administered to a knight-aspirant when being dubbed a full-fledged & pledged knight
Scooched < from scooch, to move over; in this tense: moved over
Sconce < another word for noggin
Cobblebones < a common material used to pave roadways on Fornia ~ usually the crushed bones of roadkills & other losers
Catgut & Horsehair < generic stitching threads used by barbersurgeons to sew sutures; still in wide usage by sawbones
Femmen < women > femman: woman; both terms laud the feminine

A dragonflight of fancy fills the smokechoked chamber ~ cressets flash flamelaps of chimeric proportions licking the groined ceiling with pop-snaps of whiplashes. A horde of face-blurred shadowy figures huddle like agaric mushrooms on the sinister side of the hall ~ cloaked & cowled, heads bowed. Sulphurous incense wafts in fog wisps ~ adumbrating the flooring as a pair of spiked spurs fly thru the shroud & clink a jinglejangle before disappearing into the realm of invisibility. A-kneeling, a lad armcrosses his chest as a knight afoot, armed-at-all-points, both-handedly overhelms a sword & swooshes ~ the colée *is* dealt & *felt!*

The lad awakens ~ *not as a man!* It knows a blow has laid it low.

Squiggling, it is a hapless worm encased in a foul-aired cocoon.

The warmth of fresh churned mud ~ *or is it blood?!* ~ is raw & sweet from the pulse upon its mouthpiece. It squirms in the pitchblack trackless void of its... its *treefall?*

It tries to remember: 'twas like riding on a puff of wind, & then, a thud, & then another gust, dewinding ~ breathtaking ~ thudthudthud. A thud still echoing.

Where is this place? What is it I am?

Another cerebration: the swish of something ~ swooping from the *sky?! What sky?*

Two rams collide! Memory or metaphor?

Something shiny, as seen thru tiny holes, advances & recoils.

A metallic tinge tingles its tastebuds. What is it?

It hears no sounds & yet feels a sensation. It is *moving!* Dragged?

To where?

For what purpose?

It wiggles in its outerskin & can not get out. Entrapped by one thing, scooched by another ~ it is more than hapless. 'Tis helpless.

It feels a turn of its sconce! Its head is being ripped off!!!

A jaw breaks! Lucency bedazzles!

Faces ~ only faces, disembodied ~ stare with eyes aflame, in anger? Or alarm? Their jaw joints move ~ showing teeth & tongue. Not a sound emerges from their mouths ~ silent is their mode of talk. Mutterers of muteness...

Darkness, all is darkness.

A blanket!? I don't need a blanket!!
'I' ~ I am not an 'it'!

Clumpityclump, clumpityclump...

Movement.

Why am I moving?

I can not move.

Clumpityclump, clumpityclump...

Wait, wait! I know these sounds ~ 'tis the sound of cartwheels, cartwheels on cobblebones ~ clumpityclump, clumpityclump...

Where are they wheeling me to?

"Whoooahh!" comes from unseen sources, a whisper upon the wind.

"Wake up ~ wake up, Sire!"

"Shhhssup, let 'im sleep."

"Look ~ his eyes open!"

"Be off with ya, now ~ you can do him no goodwill here!"

"Will he *live?*"

"That's more than I can say for the likes of you ~ dimwit! Tend to the horse, squire! Now, let me mend the torse. Dehorsed is *all* he is. & *what* a joust! He dehisced yon Unred *what's-a-Sir* ~ 'e's better off a headless corpse."

The Rainbow Bird appears ~ a flaming sword in its talons. Its gloriously nacred hued wings spread-eagle across the arc of the nebbia ~ the Disc the spot where it alights.

Nimble in the ways of war & amends ~ with sword as needle & shield as thimble ~ it sews catgut & horsehair into symbols athwart the smokechoked sky:

> *With this sword,*
> *who shall*
> *I smite*
> *to make*
> *wrongdoers*
> *take to*
> *flight?*

The sword is castdown into a black forest. The mightiest of the giantry trees trembles, topples: axed as if a blade of scythed grass.

The smoldering sword burns its blade into the treerings of the trunk. The 's' is taken away from the tip of the 'sword' & placed behind the hilt. Thusly, *sword* becomes *words.*

A knight in rusted iron offsaddles a crowbait. The ride now over, glue becomes its hide.

Hammerman's steel takes up the woodcutter's work. A wheelwright is summonsed, old armor his pay. A woodworker's reward is handcarted away ~ clumpityclump, clumpityclump...

A school of femmen ~ an eyeful of evedom in the flesh, unabashed ~ swim clearwaterly past a jester in a mirror'd pool as still as glass. The lips of the nymphs turn into fish-kisses & limbs & luscious skins change to scales & fins. The tranquil translucent liquid ferments in an eyewink ~ diosmosing into eructations, toad belches, malodorous mirkmuck ooze: a bubbling badwater spa.

 A geyser sprays the lilypond with spittle.

 A green foam rings the slough-edge sludge.

 Dragonbugs buzzfly the jester, sour-turn into road-apples ~ creating a dungheap.

 Slithy things, unbefore seen, do filthy things & tulips wilt into tule-tubes.

 Swamp gas glows an eerie glowth.

 Nothing grows same-o-same-o growth.

 Muckducks ~ drakes, hens & *-lings* ~ eating wermin *(yuk!)* slime into the *yick!* they pluck.

 The ceaseless winds stop & the air stales.

 Puke green tincts the whole sick scene. No other offcolour can be seen.

 The quickmire ground bloats like a bullfrog.

 Aqua recedes into mudpuddles.

 The stagnant stench reeks worse than decay.

 E'en bumblebugs mumble 'bout the worsening conditions & gasp in exasperation!

 Stinkslugs & skunk *ughs!* are the only things breathing easy.

 The jester laments a dirge.

Mares lassoed in the light oft lead to a herd of snares in the pit of night. The day dawns none too soon...

The man stretches, yawns & eye-opens to the scents of his nasal sense. "Bedamn, raven, your haven here smells like a dunghole warmed over!" he says, passing the blame.

Hmmm ~ thinks he, uncooked fish & river-rat lifestyles don't fit into my eyesocket scheme of things.

"Raven?"

The bird does not answer.

The man looks around & sees his predicament ~ what was bankside before nightrise & is not at dawnfall, is now a sandbar.

Kaw kaw comes the raven 'cross the moat.

Little rivers ceaselessly change, surmises the man, & yet, this one seems, somehow, some *why* ~ strangely familiar.

Wading kneedeep thru the water & scampering up a red clay embankment, he eyeviews a rustic pasture & conjures up a rusty thought ~ *could that be the mound I dug so long ago?*

The raven darts up & fluts down upon his shoulder & shrugs.

The man walks softly o'er to the grassy knoll & kneels. A long moment of silence passes. He arises & says to the winds "Rest sword, rest; no services of arms, need I, on my lifequest."

The man treks on, not looking back.

9
THE CROWKEEPERS' CROFT

Castle ruins
Paint picturesque
Landscapes...
Backgrounds
Make for feeble
Placesettings...
Taint a diff'rent light:
A snug hearth
In a crozy croft
& a haybed in a loft
Is oft more quietsome
& welcome
Than a petty kingdom.

Fictionairy

<u>Dolmen</u> < cromlech; the long lost-art of stonehenge-ing, no longer articulated
<u>Motte</u> < the mound made with the dirt heaped up from digging thy moat
<u>S'Kcirtap Castle</u> < Patrick's Eltsac
<u>Topiary</u> < 1. 'art' of trimming & training trees & shrubbery into unnatural shapes 2. the next craze
<u>Cocksfoot</u> < not uncommon orchard grass
<u>Handicured</u> < worked with handheld shears
<u>Escalade ladder</u> < ancient device for scaling castle walls; more or less replaced by more portable grappling irons (or hooks)
<u>Husb</u> < the male counterpart in a wedknot without the *-and*
<u>Een</u> < plural of 'eye'

The Dolmen In The Glen 'arches' like a gate & is said to bring good luck upon those who pass under, except it is nearabouts the Middle of Nowhere & hardly anyobody enters... The man does. The raven does not. It bids adieu with a caw & crowflaps away. The man waves, knowing where he is going ravens are ravished & relished. He eyesright to a yon motte ~ sighs. The trefoil-shaped keep of S'Kcirtap Castle, an aeon ago besieged, sapped, rammed & delieged ~ he thinks, looks well entwined in vines.

He comes upon an orchard of crowberry trees ~ hundreds, marching in inanimate precision, row upon row. Every *noirberry* bush is trimmed well ~ in topiary-fashion ~ mostly in farmfolk forms, caricatures of people, domestic bestials. The shubbery looks more like scarecrows than *real* scarecrows ~ which is what they aren't.

'Tis no secret: scarecrows *attract* crows as sure as statues bewitch turtle-doves.

The man knows this well ~ as well as he knows this place.

He beelines straight down a cocksfoot path heading for a cottage tucked away deep inside the handicured groves.

He even makes a point to dust off his cape & affix the feather in his hat a wee bit neater.

He knocks upon the cottage door three times in quick succession.

Mistress Crowkeeper answers & he gains admission.

She's the most roundish woman e'er imagined & jus' as huggable as most femmen. Says she "Glorybe, mymy, meme, Giraffle, lookcomesee, i'st The Tree Thinner." She says this as he tries to embrace her. Alas, his lanky arms are not near enough long enough.

Giraffle gets up out of his chair & towers o'er the man. "Heya, Trim!" says he & adds "welcome, welcome back!!" Giraffle's as tall as any escalade ladder can be.

The guest says "Come on now, call me Willbe The Word-Burner."

The Crowkeepers will have none of it.

"Tree Thinner," speaks the roundish woman, "you look so thin, bo', ya gotta have some of *my* crowmeat & crowberry pie!"

"Trim," asks Master Crowkeeper to the man as he ushers him into a chair by the fireside, "you ain't still pondering to be a dangdern book varmit, now are ya? Give it up, bo', t'ain't no *future* ~ hangitup with the ole Bicch & all. Ya ought to go in with me, bo', heckya, next to me you're the best Tree Trimmer 'round. Want to go in biz, bo'?"

Before he can respond...

"Thin," says the roundish woman rolling in a hogshead of meade "now, drink this up, bo' ~ we'll all aneed it aturned over for a table by sup." Handing him & her husb dunking cups she barrels out before he can even be polite, with *words.*

"Trim, ya ought to think 'bout my offer," he continues "& drink on it. Tree Trimming is go'n to be the next craze."

"Thin, want a baker's dozen or jus' twelve of *my* pies?" his hostess asks as she wheels in a wooden workbench, snapping crow's heads & kneading dough.

"Trim ~ he'll take *two* dozs. of *your* pies, Pinksy," answers Giraffle for his lil buddy.

Tween 'Trim' & 'Thin' & tin cups of meade ~ & ne'er a word in edgewise ~ & ten courses of crow' & 'berry pie, the rest of the dawe & most of the eve was a blurry vision to the man's een.

Sometime, a lil afore or after the witching hour, he nosedived into his eleventh pie.

Giraffle, without benefit of hoist, lifted him up to his rafter berth.

Pinksy, in her roundish femmenly mirth & laughter, tucked him in his joist bedchamber.

He dream*ethed* the dream*th* of a Ne'erending Cup.

Came cockcrow ~ or here, the crowcaw of morn. The man overslept.

Midside of day, the man awoke & poked his headache up. Down again it went, & he.

Later he arose, still bloodshot, red-nosed.

Mistress Crowkeeper kept last night's pies & placed 'em in a basket for 'im.

"Many thanks," he got out stumbling thru the doorway.

"Mymy, byebye, do be back soon, Thin..."

Master Crowkeeper was out in the fruitary, scooping up the crows of the day with his long-handled net when they met.

"Trim," said Giraffle as he scraffled with his prey of birds "don't give up the word-burn'n."

"Thanks, I won't," said he, stumbling on.

10
THE
WINDY
WAY

The wind whips
Like a slap
On the back
Along
The Windy Way ~
The only via
Tweesh De Citi & El Lay.

Fictionairy

<u>Tweesh</u> < between atwixt & ytwyn
<u>Addle-in-the-noggin</u> < fuzzybrained
<u>Anhelations</u> < how not to breathe; shortness of wind, as in pantings
<u>Evanescent</u> < exact opposite of everlasting whilst still being this side of neverneverwas
<u>Awk</u> < the direction of, as in -*ward*
<u>Guisard-masquers</u> < disguise-maskers > as in masters of disguise.
   † *good examples:* thespians, angels & readers
   †† *bad examples:* unreads, illiterates & Unreds, highway robbers, waylayers, painted ladies, con artists, alms askers, cult leaders, & others too disguised to debunk
<u>Coggles</u> < co*bb*les with *gg*
<u>Greenthumboneship</u> < godsupsoneship on a low-bred scale
<u>Plowed Prore</u> < plowed prow (?) > figure of speech implying 'one's nose is in the dirt' (¿?)
<u>Akimbo</u> < akin to kimbo, also misspelled akemboll, akenbold & arm-angled > what an idler does when something else should be done: place one's hands on one's hips & stand; usually said of strawbosses

In his footloose-bootabout way, the man, still addle-in-the-noggin, respiring with anhelations, finally runs into The Windy Way ~ *the* road. He beseems to have half-forgotten how windy it is along this meandering swath thru Fornia. As his cape flaps up like a lassy's skirt kicked up too high to hide what's 'neath the drapery, he holds unto his floppy hat & wind-bends into the roundabout direction of De Citi. He looks neither hither or thither nor eyers out towards a thicket of briars across the path. On nigher eyescan he'd have seen a sheen of something glitt'y shimmering for an evanescent winkyblink from the brush.

As he struts along, the windsy airs seem to lie down a bit with each long stride. 'Tis because The Windy Way is indenting away from The Ledge-Edge ~ the ragged hemline of 'the coast' (never capitalized) where most Fornians assume that Fornia ends. At least on this side of the world.

The Windy Way winds inland for no other sense of aimless purpose than to be the most scenic & indirect route betwixt two distinct & distant destinations.

Oft no more than a foot&hoof path, the road is as awk to journe upon as the countryside is awe inspiring to gaze on.

Scenic beauty is a fallacious mistress.

As misleading as The Windy Way is, it is no place for soft shoulders.

'Tisn't jus' the offchance dropby of guisard-masquers 'hind every rock & arbor. 'Tis the Right O' Way Law & the custom. Maybe, laws are token ~ customs shan't be broken!

The rules of the road are simple: yield or wield; as in step aside or contest the crossing. It matters not if the traffic is oncoming or comingon.

How else to regulate the route? To take to the road one risks the horns.

On Fornia, wherever the pavestones begin & end, no matter which-a-gravel one travels, its coggles are paved in cobblebones.

No cobblebones or other improvements cover the road surface nearabouts here. 'Tis much too close to the Equidistance of Nowhere. Not enough trade out this far to keep hiway-robbery a respectable hobby.

Neither El Lay nor De Citi have a legit writ to commerce or converse with t'other. What's one Walled In Town got that the other does not? Besides, charters, for starters, can easily be bonfired if no bonafide reason to raise a Wall Tax were ever found out. De Citizens & El Laybackers would raze their walls if ever was thought some commonground tween them.

Roadside, the hills seem smoother, the man thinks, than in his past few days. More round, now, like fair maidens. Then he envisions a milken cow. Derndang ~ should've kept those crowmeat & crowberry provisions Pinksy left-over for me! Why'd I leave 'em with Giraffle on my way out?

On doublethought, he shrugs off the visions of birdpies dancing in his groggy noggin.

On third thinkover he ails for some ale.

'Tis easy to be foggy-minded, midday after a dream of ne'erending pails of meade.

Aloud & to himself says he, "I despise crow' & 'berry pies!" He means it.

Overhead, Disc dots are chasing after cloud-fleece. The day, already mostly wasted in bed, is fast turning to eve.

In this seemingly serene setting along The Windy Way, roadsided with open fields of green grasses & windflowers ~ e'en Discflowershields ~ the man beseems to be getting close to his homeground. When the road abruptly turns into a cartwheel rutted track ~ giving the false impression of a twolane bridlepath ~ the man instinctively hops over to his dexter side of the road. He eyes the tuff of turf growing down the centre 'dividing' isle of the trail as if a gardener surveying his greenthumboneship.

After a hooked swerve & rise in the road, The Windy Way beelines thru a vale greener & less hilly. Soakwoodia trees are much more numerous, grouping together in woodstocks. Not one of the gnarled, wind-blownt veggies seems to be playing solitaire.

Walkabouts can be great exercise, providing one looks about & takes adequate precautions. Perhaps because he's strolling thru familar turf he lets his mind wander. Or thinks with his feet. Midway 'cross the dale he trips in a pothole, nosediving into the roadbed.

Most major accidents are more or less avoidable. Minor mishaps usually are the greatest of pitfalls. Ordained, perchance, by providence.

Caution kills ~ the man thinks, savoring the lack of flavor in a mouthful of road dirt, knowing he should have been watching where he was going.

'Tis a wonder isn't it, how when one is down nothing seems to align up with one's bellyflop?

Funny, too, how even the wind likes to kick up dust in one's plowed prore.

Heavier things than air tempt the wind.

The winds brisk up & whisk up his hat afore he has the chance to upright his decumbent bonebag. The floppy hat graces midair with a newfound freedom & attempts a sloppy stunt of flying, & flops.

He raises his head & shakes his noggin; it swills a bit but doesn't rattle.

His floppy hat aplumed with the feather pen, drops a few armslengths away from his prone body.

Turning half on his backside, he half sits up & checks for blood on his lips & cheeks. None. He spits & eyes the crimson spittle. Hmmm ~ he shoulder shrugs, so he tooth-cut his tongue a little.

The man probes his mouthpiece with a fore-fingertip before he realizes the breathing winds are teasingly scooching his hat ~ that & the quill pen, two of his most prized possessions.

The hat skitters.

He haunches up on his hind legs & leapfrogs for his headpiece.

It hops away.

He lunges again as it skipropes high enough to escape his grope.

Defeat by an unseen, ghosty nemesis not being his prime objective, the man resorts to the tactic of stealth to reclaim his belongings.

Unfortunately, unlike a daisylion graceful on the prowl ~ a feline four&surefooted predator agile from paw to claw ~ this two-leggy hero is forced to stoop to crawl. Edging closer to his prey, elbowjoint to kneecap, high tail in the air, he crouches towards the prize. Waiting for a lull in the wind ~ he pounces just as it bounces & takes aflight.

The feather pen flitters away from the hat & takes to the breeze with all the fairylike ease of an untethered kite. The quill ~ devoid of penblood in its vein ~ flutters midair in somersaults & acrobatics more whimsical than the antics of colourflies ~ until it gains the height of blustery streamers & becomes so wind-borne & wind-blownt as to overfly the sky!

Long minutes pass as the wayfarer stares into the emptiness of the pink & rouge nebbia. He sighs as if he's mourning the loss of a langsyne friend ~ not jus' the wind whisked away flight of a plume pen. An empty pen, eyed first by a raven, no less, no more, only a few days before.

Regaining his feet, he stands akimbo, lapping his wounded tongue 'gainst his inner lips. Seen is a man, licked by next to nothing at all.

11
NIGHT
ON THE
STUMP STOOL

Who has ne'er
Awoken in a strange bed
& said
'Was last night for real?'
No need to play the fool
Unless you've
Spent a night
Sit-sleeping
On the stump stool.

Fictionairy

Battel < another form of battle
Fustian < mostly useless
Anenst < toward (?)
Reccheles < totally reckless
Purloiner < thief
Purlieu < old form of neighorbood, back when there was such a thing
Pontis of Time < bridge of time > an imaginary form of reckoning, even when all roads led to... *somewhere* (!?!)
Maugre < 1. Shak. form of 'notwithstanding' (?) 2. a wife's common stance on her husb's opinion 3. a defi*ant* stance
Morth & Murdum < Poet-talk for death & murder when battelgore still made for good bardic recital
Biolysis < 1. a clinically-cleaned-up word for *death* 2. the nature of thing's way of all flesh
Tarsi < the 'foot' on the leg of an insect & some *arthropods* ~ the latter probably being just bigger bugs
Tump < woodstock
Aurum & argenium < drossy rocks, much sought after
Drossy < mostly useless

The man aims the bowstring sight of his eyes closer aground & beholds his hat: wind-tossed into the arm-branches of a nearby soakwoodia tree. Dusting himself off, he neverminds the battel alost & the loss of the fustian plume. He oscillates his hatless head anenst the tree & its arborhood of neighbors ~ espyingly ~ as if to discern any dangers inwith the woodstock. Bootheeling off the road, he proaches easylike, anigh The Hat Catcher Tree. The gnarled giant isn't about to spook. It does not even quiver its leafy headdress.

On close approach, the man see his reccheles probe. This is not just an anyoday ole 'woodia ~ this is a withy Hat Catcher. He eyerolls his orbballs as he peers up & catches a glimpse of all the hats this monster has caught: helmets & headpieces of every description, toques, caps & hoods beyond redemption, hats of e'ery make & weftage ~ felt, fur, straw, hide, cloth & fluthe, feather & scale to name a few!!! Even a crown or two!!! All entwined in its leafage & boughage.

"Excuse me, Sire," the man says as he bows in front of the trunk of the hatnapper "hats of numberless quantity & quality you do own. All I ask of your Majest, Tree, is the one not yet grown into ye. 'Twas thrown by the wind ~ but only on loan."

The tree does not answer. The tree does not one thing.

Raising himself from his humble posture, he eyes the branch that has snatched his hat. 'Tis too high to reach without an escalade ladder & yet it's on its least lofty branch.

The man walks away from the unrelenting purloiner & goes about reconnoitering the shady purlieu. Finding few sources of aid, he returns with what he hopes will make due: a flat rock & a twiggy faggot. The former a formidable missile, he hopes. The latter not nearly long enough a lance to reach the branch.

"Tree," the man declares "brigand tree that thou art, 'tis your last chance ~ before I war upon thy branch: surrender my hat!"

The Hat Catcher Tree says & does nothing.

He javelins the twig to release his hat. It misses the mark, splintering into an overfall of slivers as it ricochets off the tough bark of another branch.

The rock is thrown & hits the hat. The hat swings & doesn't fall. Neither does the rock. It sticks to the selfsame bough as holds his hat, held in place as if by some sticky sap.

The Hat Catcher Tree awakes from a nap. It quavers its treetop. A cascade of overgreeny foliage filters down, inundating the man & the ground. Not one headpiece is released in the leaf-fall deluge.

At wits' end & up to his armpits in leaves, the man backfights his way out of the pile & retreats to a stump stool a few paces away & sits to ponder on his problem.

The Hat Catcher Tree stretches deep, deep down into its roots & thinks ~ ummm, I don't want that greenless, rootless, water-sap of a tumblebush weeding on my Seeder's grave!

All the other gnarled giant soakwoodia trees living in this woodstock venue, clumped around the sacred stump ~ now desecrated by this Seederless weed ~ think similar thoughts.

The weed knows not what it is doing.

'Tisn't easy to be gutsy & a tree.

Why bark out one's inner feelings when it's so easy to hide behind the thick outercovering of expressionless woodskin?

None of the trees speaks up, & yet, as they go about sopping up their thoughts in quietude, each soaks up & is nurtured by the cerebrations of the multitude.

In a short time, The Hat Catcher Tree drops the weed's weedtop. By noncoincidence, the hat plops into the soggiest, muckiest mudpuddle around.

To the powwow in the deepest recesses of the spongebog rootsystem, to the root-hairs of each soakwoodia tree's wet-cell batteries, came the same spark of thought: to get rid of the infestation, give it back its headdress.

The man hears the *splish!* of the splash & eyes his hat in the muck. Getting up off his rump, he walks over to the *splat!* & picks up his hat. After examining it inside & outside, the man wringdries it as best he can. Walking back, he hangdries it on a knot of the stump!

To the entire arborhood's outrage & bewilderment, the weed returns to its original position on the sacred stump!!!

The soakwoodia trees rustle their leaves in a furious rage ~ wildbeasts rattling a cage ~ to nil avail.

The man doesn't know he belongs in jail.

Looking up at the treetop bustle, the man perks up a smirk ~ he thinks the wind is doing to the leaves the same-o treatment done to him with such ease.

Soon the trees simmer down & return to the seep of thoughts.

Thinks The Hat Catcher Tree ~ the hardest block of thud 'tisn't wooden.

Another, with more rings 'round its girder, reflects: insects *this* size haven't been *bzzzing* by in myomy ~ how long?!

The man, enthroning himself upon a sacred shrine ~ a tomb, no less ~ all too soon begins to doubt the existence of Hat Catchers. Thinks he: proximity is everyothing ~ a tree near a road is bound to snare the wind-blownt off wares of passer-byers. O'er the Pontis of Time ~ the wind blows all portage away.

Dusk is rising. The early ground-fog of eve jinnis out of the porous subsurface of Fornia.

The man concedes to another night lost away from *home* ~ now, only a half day walkup The Windy Way.

To while away the good-gloom remaining of the dawe, he pulls out his penknife & begins to carve frufra etchings into the deadwood stump of the half-petrified tree he rumps upon. He is stumped *why* the *wood* is so *hard* to *work!* The task soon takes up the efforts of both his hands ~ dern handuscript *you'd* make, inkles he.

The man soon tires of penknifing & retires to the sanctity of an oncoming umpth.

'Tis just as well. Already he has stripped the stump of most of its bark, all of its dignity.

Hunchbacking o'er, he props his head up hand to chin, elbowjoint to kneecap. T'other arm rests 'cross straddling thighs. Eyeclose comes easy. In a wink he's sit-sleeping upon the defaced stump.

Soon afterwards, the penknife stuck into the stony wood keels over ~ missing his boots & their leather-covered guardians. It falls to the ground in silentness, dumb to its crimes.

The all enshrouding cloud of nightrise climbs to obscure the last remaining traces of the vanishing Disc ~ erasing all vestiges of vision.

Mummingbirds huddle into the nestlings of the conveniently pouched sanctuaries of The Hat Catcher Tree ~ ssshhhing their young'n birdies no bigger than a bumblebug with soft whispered stories of oldentime glories: before the advent of races of egg-robbers & owl-eyes.

Cricket bands begin to fiddle with their bow-legs.

The winds, bored with bloring the lower-tune trumpets of sweeping the carpet, raise their tones to the buglecry of the rooftop sky.

Other things awaken...

Things beyond the scope of eyes.

Beings beyonder the grips of probers.

The Queen of the red, firebite-antler ants ~ the fieriest biters on Fornia ~ by no accident lives with her underants within the crannies of the tree stump the trespassing giant is sitting upon. Like any infuriated Queen, she's furious! Afteritall, it is serious business to deal with an uninvited behemoth. Especially so when it has chiseled away at one's rooftop & torn most of the tiles off one's walls!

Without using words, the Queen queries her daughters ~ antly communicating instead with chemical erotemes.

Her underants hark without hearing, maugre they understand her questions. Immediately the underants answer their Queen by all volunteering.

They respond by attacking one another. Each vies for the honour of being the first red, firebite-antler ant to bite The First Bite!

The sororal legion of underants firebite & antler each other in a free-for-all melee of mass havoc & deathpile mess ~ altho, on a somewhat miniature scale.

The Queen bides her time by passing more anteggs while her daughters bite & antler their sisters.

Sis-'gainst-sis, the civil war rages with all the fury of gorious morth & murdum, the sib squabble made all the more a redfest by the excuse to commit sororicide: an inbred notion.

Soon the merely mathematical question is answered by the simplest military equation ~ subtract the number of those not adding up to the sum of what's leftover.

The aftermath is obvious to the Queen. Her house is divided into those bitten to death & those antlered to biolysis.

Thus, with her numeral strength depleted by the quest to be the biter of The First Bite & for the simple reason that there are no longer any living red, firebite-antler underants to carry out her request, the Queen wisely decides to hold back the assault on the giant until another batch of anteggs hatch.

The Queen, exhausted after watching all the ruckus over The First Bite, fatigued by having to clean up her nest ~ by eating all the dead underants & toothpicking out their exoskeletons ~ drained by having laid another generational cluster of anteggs, yawns. She falls asleep clutching as many of her brood as her antler antennae & six-legs & five-segmented tarsi can touch.

Around the stump, every timber of the tump is sapping up peaceful thoughts ~ save one, The Hat Catcher Tree. It's frantically throwing every headpiece in its collection to the high-blowing winds, in the mistaken belief that this act of penance will make the weed sitting on its Seeder's stump go away.

Nearby the desecrated stump, a shamerock is lifting up its spirits by rocking itself over. Unfortunately, in doing so, it bowls over a clump of mushstumps & stumpstools.

Nothing should be taken for granite ~ this poor shamerock was not always a worthless boulder.

Once, more than a stone's age ago, it was worshipped & held in awe. It was part of a cromlech on a near but distant world.

A falling moonstone fell upon its plain one day & the *L* of the crom/ech got knocked into orbit.

After roaming the outermost part of the outer Atmos for more revolutions than can be finger-counted, a strange thing happened to the proud slab of stone: it changed into a flaky nugget of aurum & argenium.

Sadder still, the once highly beheld & hefty megalith fell to Fornia ~ a fallen rock!

Yea, many a Fornian has sat upon its shiny skin ~ oblivious to the wheal's worth of what they sat upon. Albeit, worthless is its weight on Fornia.

Fornia abounds with glitt'y & crystals & has lil use for sparkl'y stuff.

For all practical purposes, flaky things like common shamerocks are only used by tinkers of cookware & makers of toys.

Fornia has a haughty attitude towards rocks!

Drossy globs of common clods are only good for keeping petty craftworkers in useless jobs ~ 'tis the general opinion.

Fornians build bridges & castles & homes out of things that can rust! Rocks that bust are what Fornia lusts!

Ashamed of what & where has befallen its fate, this shamerock ~ like so many others of its vein ~ has been rocking & rolling for so long in search of some sense of selfworth, it has got pebbles for brains.

This foolish shamerock, what does it expect ~ rolling stone fame?

How can anything so common be considered so great?

The only billing these blockheads can obtain are the shieldsign warnings: Bewareth O' Fallen Boulders.

More common, less than nothing to do with shamerocks: Wayfarers Beitknown ~ Ye Travel On *so&so's* Cobblebones. Or: **X** Soft Shoulders.

If this shamerock really wishes to find its way, it needs a sense of direction. If it truly wants to rollover The Ledge-Edge, it's rocking to the wrong flipside. 'Tis heading deeper into the Inferior! Eventually, it'll roll into the interior of The Oblong Valley ~ one huge open-air amphitheatre.

From the crater to the gravel pit, a shamerock leads a less than meteoric existence.

First comes the false dawn. It comes upon the illusion of a liftdown in the shroud of night. 'Tis only caused by the commotion in The Hat Catcher Tree.

Next comes the first impression of the impending daybreak: the cloud of night falls into a thick ground-fog.

As the last wisps of fog seep into the porous airlandic substratum the dawe opens.

First is heard the chirp of birds ~ minus the finest birdsong of the mummingbirds.

Poppies pop open their petals like eyelids.

Windflowers unwind their windsweep tincts of colours.

Discflowershields veil their frail faces with leaves ~ preferring the dew of nightrise to the Disc of dayfall.

The flutterbys & fairybugs take to the buzzz of their biz.

Other critters follow.

Furrytails scurry & hop along.

This day, like all others, begins in a hurry.

The song of the auroral winds is voiced in bursts ranging from pianissimo to fortissimo.

Something dawns on the sit-sleeping man as he half-slumbers on the stump stool, altho, by the time he bestirs 'tis way past dawn. He yawns & awakes to an a-pleasing umpth ~ a sound only heard in his inner ear. As usual, the sound keeps him from getting up.

Oft the umpth, he thinks, makes him hard of hearing. In truth, he is simply hard of listening. He can not describe the sound of an umpth ~ he has tried until it hurts. At times, he believes the umpth sounds like a rustle of leaves & at other moments he truly hears an inner voice edging him on. What's worse ~ he feels the umpth a curse! With this thought there comes an

        u
        u
        u
        u
        U
        M
        P
        T
        H

Approaching sounds are overheard, he thinks. Then he thinks he thinks too much. Yet, even over the umpth of his life, he hears it anon.

Rubbing his eyes, as in wonderment, the man gets up off the stump & tries to peer thru the underbrush. To his surprise, an unlikely traveler comes a-walking down The Windy Way!

12
THE
HAGGARD WOMAN
AND THE
RAINBOW MAN

An ol' woman &
A featherweight man
~ what commonground
Can they meet upon?
Volumes of words
Will come tween them
Afore any correlation
Can be found...

Fictionairy

Toggery < apparel
Cowlstaff or Shillelagh < when walking sticks were in fashion & had names
Ort < crummy table scraps
Termagant < 1. an imaginary deity 2. a hag 3. some bag-ladies
Grimalkin < a cat spirit
Cudgeling < to beat with a cudgel, in this case ~ a walking stick
Skedaddling < opposite of *saber charging!*
Weazen < beanpole skinny
Gangleshank ↑ same as above, more so
Bullwacker < 1. a bullwhip (?) 2. one who wacks bulls (??)
Bothy < a home, of sorts
God < a mouth, usually a big one
Lissome < 1. same as lithesome 2. nimble

The man takes a good, long looksee at an old biddy talking away ~ to *herself?!* ~ as she's walking nearer. Her toggery seems off some bargain rack of a *used-once* haberdashery. A bit ragtag, & yet, too hot-ironed & tidy to be the garb of a hag living out of a bag! She's shawled, wearing the headscarf like a babushka veil. Her footwear sandals, her socks kneetops. She hobbles along on a cowlstaff or shillelagh. In one hand The Haggard Woman is holding orts & tossing tidbits to something *yet* unseen. Thru the briars the man takes note: the vagrant termagant is feeding a grimalkin & chanting her mumbojumbo ~ "*Cumon taddy abby, dono beso crabby, dono askme whywhywhy!*"

The man steps o'er the shamerock & walks unto The Windy Way. "What's that?" asks he of The Haggard Woman, pointing to the four-footed furrytail.

This headlong confrontation with the before unseen man startles the old woman. She eyes the stranger with suspicion & much apprehension. The air fills with suspense. The furry cat quivers a question mark tail.

"What is that?" requestions the man.

"That," The Haggard Woman answers in a voice broombooming of crony witchwifery *"that is a who! Who happens to be a Question Mark Cat! Be off with ya, now or I'll give ya a good cudgeling I shall!"* These last words she adds after tossing whatever it was in her hand at the the man's torso & raising her walking stick like a weapon.

"I don't *believe* in Question Mark Cats," the man replies, taking no defense nor showing any offence.

"I don't give a hoot whatcha believe! Scooch over & let me pass!" says she picking up the cat & trying to walk crane-distance around the man.

He stands aside & lets her pass.

"Just ya stay where's ya are," scowls The Haggard Woman prodding her cowlstaff in menacing swordplay & making doublesure that her backside isn't exposed to the *brigand-man!*

Asks he to the skedaddling hag, "Don't happen to have any penblood on your person by chance ~ or better still, a plume pen afilled, that I may purchase?"

The Haggard Woman turns 'round to facedown this oddball inquisitor. She flings a volley of poisontipped words, "What bar-sinister name of wierdo yield-or-wield game are ya playing, boy? How dare you affright an old lady on a lonely stretch of this wretched road!?! You scare my poor feline friend!!! You, *you!*, have the gall to extorterize me for such a useless thing to the likes of *you!* ~ a pen! You fiend!! You scum!!! What sect of low-bred mom does a crumb like you puke forth from!?! Did your sheep-flocker of a pa hitch-up with the halter of some cow? I'st fearful to me, a poor aged wench, to have to smell your stinky pigsty stench!!! Ah, what & such filth crops up from the illth that bad seeds do so sow!!! Go now, be off, hide your vile mug back in the tree-swinging hideout you sprang from!!! Go back to your weald of cowards or tend to your drove of weazen, gangleshank cowherds or whatever was your sleazen reason driving ya to such a lowly pit!!! Ya think *I* don't know your ilk!?! You're not a man: you're a branworm! Go squirm, milktoast, Bibliowermin, you are worse than the Bicch!!!! Scamp off nit, lice of wit, before I pluck from my purse a curse ~ hex, vex & X you!!!!!"

The man is simply overawed, enthralled & unerringly bewitched by this heady wordplay performance & patiently awaits an intermission ~ not out-facing to interrupt such a rhapsody of footloose at the mouthing!! A pause in her cusses offers his cue & he applauds by croising forefingers into an X ~ the handsign of *yield*.

She smirks at this token of respect, rendering a curtsey.

He bows ~ a-kneeling ~ in the very middle of the tuff of turf amid The Windy Way & says "Milady, forgive me, your Grace, into your service I do avow ~ yet do sheathe thy tongue or sharpen thy unwhetted wit! You are neither a witch ~ 'cause I've known some ~ nor e'en a spinster bibliomarm ~ tho thou dost admit to have charmed *one*. Nay, milady, this plumeless featherweight, bonedry of penblood, bids you faire greetings from dangdern-nearabouts the Equidistance of Nowhere & begs you no harm."

The Haggard Woman is quite impressed by this gest...

When The Brun Girl ~ bloomtime in evefruits, sloven in raiment ~ sashays by & says to the kneeling man, "Hey ya, Zipfly, glad you are back! Hope ya read to me soon!"

The man without looking up retorts "Come on by tomorrow."

The Brun Girl chasses away with a girliegoo giggle, wiggling like a wermin.

The Haggard Woman, not knowing what to make of *that,* releases the Question Mark Cat. It runs off, question tail high, to do the secret things cats privately do.

The Question Mark Cat paws off the road & cat whisker marks some flowers.

The flowers speak in a daisylion voice, *Meow maaaameeeeoooooowh! Who are you & whatcha do'n out here?*

The Question Mark Cat struts off its tail & meeewsz ~ *liiem theei* ? *liioni! Theei laaaoosti o meow liioni! Meooowh whootariuuuuuu?*

The daisylion answers ~ *Theei laaaoosti o meow liioni! Liiiki meow floooweri furri?*

The Question Mark Cat purrs, purrfuming its scent glands o'er the daisylion's fur.

The daisylion catlicks Question Mark's tail & meewsz ~ *meeow noooti o tomliioni o theei?*

The Question Mark Cat quavers her tail in a quivering ??????????????????

Me neither says the daisylion *let's go someplace full of catnap nip & fresh fish & birds too dumb to take to the wing who always sing & giveaway their whereabouts & where nothing e'er changes!!!!!!!!!*

Wowwoowah answers the Question Mark Cat & asks *where is such a place full of catnap nip & fresh fish & birds too dumb to take to the wing?????????*

They went to Where Nothing E'er Changes.

After The Brun Girl walks on, out of sight & mind, The Haggard Woman hobbles o'er to her capitulating foe. Just as she raises her cane o'er his head, wielding her baston of power...

A knight gallops up & *Whooooaaaahs!*

The Haggard Woman lowers her walking stick & leans 'gainst it. Looking up at the mounted Sire, she squints at the sight of the knight.

His armor is as rustred as iron can be without being metallicy dead. His oval shield is a field of red. His cape ~ a flowing tapestry of dusty red. E'en the crest of his rusty helmet is a streamer of red. The knight holds up a lance ~ two & a half man-size in length ~ surgeon-barber-poled in red & white.

She looksover the steed.

The charger is afoam with froth & nutty brown, *almost* red. The noble beast is saddled with red leather & blanket-draped with a flaming red skirting.

The cavalier unhelms.

His nose is red, hair aflame, bloodshot his eyes, red his neck.

He speaks, "Forgive my interruption, mihag, I am Woodright ~ a truly red knight."

She nods.

The knight then addresses the man akneeling, brows low, "Sire Cheffrey, I'm gleeful ye're back! See ya on the good-gloom o'tomorrow."

The bowed man mumbles, "Call me Willbe..."

Ignoring the man's last comments the rusted-red knight nods *ta-ta* to the hag, rehelms his redhead & horseshoes off down The Windy Way ~ hoofkicking up a cloud of reddish dust as he *hihos* away.

The Haggard Woman returns to her quarry, "Featherweight, you *say* you are, eh?! What books have you word-burned?? Speak up, man, unfold your story!"

"No books word-burned as yet, Milady, but I am word-burning one now ~ 'tis to say, I've returned to complete a book."

"Returned?" queries she, "From where??"

"In search of penblood & The Rainbow Bird," reports the man.

Hmmm ~ thinks The Haggard Woman, maybe this rogue really is a writer ~ afteritall, no two people seem to call him by any *one* name.
Wanting to hear more, she notices the man's rainbow scarf. She hmmms again. "Arise, ye plumeplucker ~ I dub thee The Rainbow Man. Up, unshield your eyes!"

The man raises to his feet & recovers his dignity. He eyes the hag straight in her face, at least the parts not covered en shawl ~ & once-overs her raggedy attire. "Milady, unless my eyes deceive me by your disguise, beneath those rags & veil, there's more curve & verve than beseems a hags! Undo your facade, this silly masquerade ~ reveal your visage!"

The Haggard Woman chuckles, almost chortles, then changes posture. She hips her hands & lets go her lips, "To look upon a hapless hag as if she were a happy hen!! Shame on such thoughts!! Aim your arrows higher & quiver thy shaft!" She thinks ~ how long has this tomcat been out here on the road!?

The man manages a blush just as an Oxman sidestraddles by on his gelded bull trying to fend off a swarming flock of buzzzflies with a bullwacker.

"Good dawe, to ye, Marse Mell," Oxman says to The Rainbow Man as he snaps a whiplash into the buzzzcloud. He hat doffs to the hag.

She nods.

"By the way," Oxman continues, "anyotime ya want me to move your ole bookcarte ~ jus' let me know."

"Thanks, I shall, see ya tomorrow," replies The Rainbow Man as the Oxman whipsnaps on.

Hmmm ~ ponders The Haggard Woman, there is more traffic here in the last few moments than I've seen in four days along The Windy Way. Eyeing all the defunct buzzzflies littered 'long the road, she asks "Rainbow Man ~ you live 'round hereabouts? Got a bothy o'er in that woodstock, have ya?"

"No & yes," retorts The Rainbow Man, "I've got a place, half a day walkup the way. Heading there, now."

The Haggard Woman wonders why a man with a house half a day away would come trodden out of a tump of soakwoodia trees. Why'd he stop when he was so close? Must be ouerve-deaf, this one, thinks she.

"You're welcome to walkalong, if ya like," The Rainbow Man offers.

The Haggard Woman half-listens to his *offer* ~ such as it is. She's more concerned about the whereabouts of her cat. She probes, "Have ya seen my Abby ~ my cat?"

"The Question Mark Cat?" asks he.

"Yea, *that* one, how many cats hang around these parts, anyoway?" she huffs & puffs.

"She ran off with a daisylion," retorts The Rainbow Man nonchalantly.

How'd he know it was a *she?!* Puzzled, she quizzes, "Did you *see* her run off, now did ya? What would *she* be doing with a wild cat??"

The man doesn't know why he knows ~ he jus' knows & changes the subject. "Going to stand in the roadway all day, asking questions about the unexplainable nature of untameable critters, are ya?"

"No, but I'm footsore," she volunteers. "I've been hoofing this road going on four days now."

"Well, if you're tired, ya can sit a-spell ~ there's a stump stool o'er in yon woods," The Rainbow Man suggests, pointing.

Dithering on the thought for a moment in hesitancy, she reconsiders ~ maybe the cat will come back if she sits awhile. "Show me," says The Haggard Woman to The Rainbow Man.
He hawkeyes the way like a good pathfinder.

"Are you *sure* there was a tree stump here?" she asks in unbelief, in the empty clearing.

"It *was* rightabout here!" the man exclaims.

"Never do mind," says she, sitting down on the shamerock, "this'll do jus' fine."

The Rainbow Man looks around to see what other pieces of nature's furniture have been rearranged. Strange ~ *very strange*, perplexes he as he scratches his hat.

She takes off a sandal & begins to massage her sore sole, foot still stockinged.

The Rainbow Man, realizing that memorizing is not a perfect art ~ altho he prides himself in ne'ver forgetting a recollection ~ concludes the boulder she's plopped on is out of place.

As The Haggard Woman rubs her toes & buffs her sock, her eyes follow what appears to be a flipflop path of squish & squash ~ it leads right up to where she sits! Headbending down to get a closer looksee at the *yickyuk!* a horror thought wormholes into her fertile burrow ~ can it be a snaily slugtrail?!

The Rainbow Man, thinking the old hag is hungry beyond the pangs of common sense & decency, shouts "Don't lick that!"

She jumps up more at the *thought* than the shout. "I'm sitting on a giant snaily bug!!!" she blurts out.

The Rainbow Man waltzes o'er & kicks the rock as she watches, shivering, holding her unsandaled foot up with her hands.

Need your crutch for that trick ~ thinks the man. "Lady, you from some Walled In Town ~ or something?! There aren't too many a-creepy gastropoddy mollucks of beforeth unbeknownt leviathan size 'round these parts ~ fact is, there aren't *any!* Besides, they'd have spirally shells! 'Tis jus' another glitt'y rock!"

The Haggard Woman scritches her itchy sock taking in the tonguelashing without much afterthought ~ & then she realizes her shawl isn't veiling her facial features. She hobbles back to the rock ~ thankful the man had his backbone to her all the while.

The Rainbow Man sits down crosslegged on the ground, not too close or far away.

Rechaired, The Haggard Woman eyes several small wonders. A lone red, firebite-antler ant is frantically anting about in the *whatever* it is exuded ooze trail. They're broken anteggs she concludes, enough to scramble up an omelette! The other stuff, smeared to smush, looks like the mush of mashed up mushstumps & stumpstools, she surmises. She resumes massaging her foot, then changes feet.

Hmmm ~ thinks The Rainbow Man, in a trance ~ bring on an umpth! This old crone is going to give me an ear-ache.

The Haggard Woman ear-sores up, "Rainbow, what'd you say you were doing here? I mean, last night?"

"I didn't say," says he. Turning towards the noisemaker he adds, "Sit-sleeping, mostly."

"No, no, *before* that. I mean, why'd ya leave the road so close to your home?"

The Rainbow Man chitchats "Well, my hat was wind-blownt into yon tree & by the time I got it back, nightrise was arising. So I doodled a bit on the *stump*... with my penknife."

"Doodled *what?*" interrupts the hag.

"Doodlenoodles, mostly," he replies & why's, "Why?"

"Got the Bicch up this way?" interrogates the inquisitive hag.

"Bicch is *everywhere!*" The Rainbow Man retorts. Then appends "Everyowhere *but, but* my book." He says these words moping.

"Why so?" asks she attentively, sitting up & reshoeing her feet.

"Ah, I'm no artist ~ least not much o' one. Hardly any illustrations or illuminations in my word-burnings. Not enough to whet the appetite of Bibliowermin, anyoway: jus' wordy pictures. Mental images don't attract the booky worms!" says he, a-sighing.

Listening to the man's anguish, The Haggard Woman wishes he would stop languishing on the Bicch. In an effort to perk him up, she ups & says, "Rainbow Man, I think the Bicch ate your tree stump!"

"Say so, who ~ *you,* an old hag?! What do *you* know about books & Bicch ~ carry 'round a tome in your lil bag, do ya, biddy?!" the man dishes out, without forking up a bit of mercy.

"Look here," says The Haggard Woman in a tone not carrying a tune of indignation, "look o'er here where I'm pointing. See that? That's a red, firebite-antler ant! These little buggers only live in old & deadwood gnarled soakwoodia tree stumps & as *every & any* one knows, this sect of treelife derndang lives next to forever!!!"

"Yea, so what?" the man mouth-shrugs.

"You know, you're more feather*brained* than a featherweight! Now, listen up. 'Cause there are few deadwood soakwoodia stumps, then there's got to be only a few red, firebite-antler ant clumps ~ right?! Rightly, so. This ant, here, is obviously quite queenly in size & demeanor. Now, what could have beaten her horde of underants & *then* eaten up her queendom?!!"

"You mean," the man popcorns out *"that, that, that, the firebite ants lost a fight! No, no, no, nonononononono ~ no way!!!!"*

"To the Bicch, no less," she professes.

The most fiery biting ants on Fornia 'twere right under *my* backside last night ~ the man mentions to himself, unaware until now, their habitat was deadwood soakwoodia stumps. By gosh, he hmmms ~ how does this hag know so much! A man can never be as old as a woman he admits ~ nor more near the marks they hit, most of the time. "Rested up, enough?" asks The Rainbow Man, standing up.

"Yep," says The Haggard Woman. "Where's this tree that trapped your hat?"

"O'er there. You can't miss it ~ it's brimful of hats!" He points towards the thiefly tree.

"Where?"

The man walks over & reaffirms his consternation & scratches his hat more than e'er.

The woman looks up at the leafless arbor & says "I don't see any hats up there & 'tis easy to eye its treetop. I think this tree is next to deadwood. Look how brittle & wilted its branches are. Poor thing probably died ten or so bloomtimes ago."

"Let's go," says the man walking towards the road.

"Are there any inns in the area?" the hag asks following in the footsteps of The Rainbow Man.

"There aren't any inns, out here," The Rainbow Man replies as he struts down The Windy Way, taking long strides.

"Oh," The Haggard Woman sighs from her shawled gob as she hobbles along on her cane.

As the two two-legged creatures tumbleweed down the turnpike out of earshot & eyesight...

The shamerock flipflops over.

Wheewh! ~ it cerebrates, glad to be relieved from the pressure that had pressed upon it.

Heave, heaveho! Another rollover. *Heaveho!* & it turns o'er again. Inadvertently, this time, the shamerock rolls over the Queen of the red, firebite-antler ants ~ the last Queen, now belated.

Thus, a distinguished species is extinguished, smished to smithers & reens, by another specie *wannabe.*

Pity the poor larvae ~ predestined to become bleachbone exoskeletons before even reaching pupahood.

Heaveto! The shamerock hears, or feels the vibrations, of something coming. It stops in its tracks ~ believing by doing so it becomes quite invisible, or something.

A knight trots up into the woodstock. Shiny his armor, oblong his shield. His colours are green. Visor down, concealed within its cocoon, the worm does not show itself. It peers thru the brambles of the bush at The Windy Way.

The horse shakes it head & shows its teeth. It *wants* to speak.

"Sssshhhhssup," the rider says to its bearer, patting the beast & pulling up the reins. They wheel about & slowly hoof away.

The arborhood of soakwoodia trees soak on deep thoughts in the spongebog.

One even knotholes sappy tears as its roots touch those of the no longer slurpstrawing Hat Catcher Tree.

It killed itself, why barkweep?

I wash my loss with teardrops of amber.

Seep on this awhile: we've lost not only our Seeder's grave ~ we've lost a treesibling who braved the winds, withstood countless ordeals of fire & fought off more infestations than any of us can shake a branch at.

Yes, but he took a part of us when he shook his lifeforce off ~ for naught.

The breeze kicks up & rustles thru the giant overgreens. In one bloring gust it snipsnaps the drywood stem of The Hat Catcher Tree. The deadwood trunk *timbers* over, crashing across the road before logrolling away.

The winds die down.

The moody thoughts of the astonished trees limber up, slowly but surely.

Lissome up, guys, quit sopping so much ~ perhaps there is a Heavenly Arboretum.

The birdsong of mummingbirds is heard.

The newly cleared spaces around the stumpy tombstone of The Hat Catcher Tree & the empty Seeder's place are bombarded with treefalls of pinecones.

Faroff, in The Oblong Valley, hats fall.

13
CIRCLE
OF
PURPLE

Sire Basilicum
Arise ye Royal Purple,
King of mint!
Rule wise with thy
Basileous scent,
Thy place is not
To bow wind-bent!
Dark Opal Ocimum
To thee we squint!
Tho not to thy
Virid cousin's tint!

Fictionairy

<u>Basilicum</u> < a Royal Upmost House of the mint family
<u>Basileous</u> < ✝ of, or, pertaining to, the above
<u>Dark Opal Ocimum</u> < upper crust of Basilicum
<u>Grubstaker</u> < a practitioner of usury
<u>Venompedia</u> < 1. poisonous reading material 2. the carpetbag contents of a *snake oil* jobber
<u>Cat & Ram</u> < oldtime machines of wardom to play cat & mouse games with
<u>En Baston</u> < barred heraldry
<u>Arriere-voussure</u> < an arch of a different form, usually over another archway, as a door or a window, & oftenly requiring a lot more brickwork
<u>Ambries</u> < *pl* of ambry ~ the original built-in appliance: a niche or cupboard in a wall

On a nearabouts hillside, a most perfect Circle Of Purple grows upon an otherwise patch of green basil backgroundcover. Bunnyhopfunnyflop, isn't it, how the mind's eye discerns such iffy abstract symbolisms? Verily, it might just be a fluke of the nature of things. For who would dare defy the Law & defile the Land ~ forbidden is the display of the Royal Emblem of the Upmost Ruling House of Fornia ~ without the right to copy, by tending such a garden? Yea ~ even here, in the Equidistance of Nowhere ~ such a crime is out of chime with established criminal practices. Out of sync or not, there it be, & yes ~ it has always been.

Since this ringlet was first run across, some langsyne olden thyme ago, this blasphemous use of the regal hued loop has been declared illegal, & has come across every conceivable abuse.

The King of Fornia ~ long before he unwedknotted the Queen, climbed off his highchair horse, cloistered himself beyond the wettest of moats & slammed the door of his throneroom behind him ~ bade this defacement be erased, obliterated & effaced from the landscape.

All mortal, mental & majestic attempts to eradicate this living legend, this weedy circ of leafy graffiti, have, thus far, utterly failed.

One may wonder why our dungeons are full; well, it all began so long ago, when none could pull up the roots of this basil bushed hill or fill the boots to stomp upon the task.

Indeed, pouts of apology & bouts of mania do not keep the keykeepers from locking you up for life & out of sight! Shouts of *"'Twasn't my fault!"* haven't e'er kept anyone out of being buried in a brickwork vault ~ a crypt for the undead losers of freewill & lively pursuits.

Verily, Royal melancholia has long set in & upon our land are cast shadowy valleys!

Truly, apathy, a seemingly incurable patheticism, rules only with the handout for alms!

We liveth in a grimy time of oily palms!

Axlegrease, wheelwrights know, slows trade.

Herbal Bueno, His Majesty's older brother, now the long dead knight e'er so colder, but then the Duke of De Citi, late-great Exchequer of the Royal Kitty & grubstaker o' many a mistaker, once undertook a plot to implant a mint crop of sages to plow asunder this offending rinc o' purple basil.

All failed, to say the least. Maist attempts do, done in haste.

To relate all the tales of failure 'twould be too word-burn-consuming to do, & wood is too precious a resource to waste on the discourse of the history of all flops. Howbeit, a good story is a commodity in any economy & three notable teasedrops are worth the penblood.

One longtoothed genius, by name of Beanius Mason-Maison de Santé, a minor Soothslayer & aleague with a major bricklayer, came up with a mortar & pestle scheme to wrestle with the amaranth: brickwall in the repulsive plants!

He bade a roundtower built upon & over the Regally illegal circ of irk! Ah, the best laid plans of measly masonic minds oft flaw! The turret sank out of sight, as if sunk in an unseen sinkhole & left without leaving a hollow. The Circle Of Purple followed up by growing a ring wider in circumference & more purple! Before Beanius could throw in the trowel he was bodily thrown into some stinkhole with a mortared-in keyhole.

Tutu Tofu II, like his natural dada before him, whom he ne'er knew, knew the flowery arts of organic husbandry. He could also walk o'er his stalks e'er so lightly & easily detect a stemmy defect ~ no matter how small or slight. 'Twas said he could tippytoe thru the gardens he grew & tendered & toesy pluck up & out any unwanted weed. He e'en claimed to know the gender of a plant by looking at the seed!!! A handucurist of the finest order, androgynous strains were his favorite grains ~ for he held them to be the purest. When it came to judging the petals of pansies he was a jurist!

In desperation the Duke turned to Tutu's inbreeding skills because he wanted to show his bro, The King, he could rid the hill of its ills.

Altho, in private, 'twas said the Duke would jus' as soon see the flowerboy dead! *Puke with perfume* the Duke is oft misquoth as heardsaid. A *fluke with legumes* is actually more accurate an example of the Dux's wordplay.

Tutu swore he'd be the apprehender of the mauve offender! He'd simply breed the purpley weeds into an infertile crop of decaying fodder.

Woebeit, for all his wilting exertions. The basil ring grew as if in perpetual bloomtime!!

Gloomtime came to Tutu in a dungeon, dark & dank. 'Tis said, so rank it stank, no one knew he was gone, until long after he was long-gone dead.

Tre d'Foil, an up & coming wonder lad of wizdomry, strove harder than most to implant a bane upon the basil bushy hoop.

He pulled from his vat all sorts of poisons, many well chosen from his voluminous venompedia of jus' such vile ointments.

He even went on to word-burn his entire lifequest of vial disappointments.

Every potion he tried ~ & he applied aplenty ~ never proved to be the right herbicide.

Fain as he was to brew up a toxin, he e'en prescribed the hoof-glue of oxen!

Waning in his efforts as he was, he changed his approach as his deadline encroached.

If the basil wouldn't die ~ he'd dye it!

He took to the alchemy of daubing in paints, yet, no paste from his palette of every tint could hide even a hint of the brazen Circle Of Purple!

As a landscape artist he was starved of success. A Royal canvasser stressed that all he was doing was making a mess. Everything he brushstroked upon the purple scene turned out to be totally useless.

The basil grew yet purple*ier*. Even the circ became more circular!

When he started to pale they smeared his reputation of *up & coming* all over his face & plastered him into some place of disgrace.

Sad his tale.

Others, too many to conjure up from the mists of obscurity, mulled o'er customized cures for this blemish on yon knoll. The feast of brainly wormholes became the diet for wermin; famish banquets of the vanquished.

Pity, moreso, the Duke of De Citi. Before he went bankrupt & abruptly died, he vied himself 'gainst the Circle Of Purple.

With drawn sword, flaming arrow, jousting lance, crossbow shaft, boiling oil, catapult, cat & ram ~ the knight fought singly on, assailing the transgressor with e'ery weapon of wardom.

E'en boisterous taunts were to no avail.

Fairly beaten ~ the warlord kneeled before the field that bested him.

'Tis said that for days before the Duke's untimely endcome at midlife, all he had eaten were boiled purple basil leaves & the plates of his shield & armor.

'Tis true, The King did truce with the Circle Of Purple, undeclared, as it may have been.

The King did declare that the *new* Royal Emblem of the Utmost Ruling House of Fornia be altered ~ *embellished* 'twere his term ~ by a purple bar *en baston*.

>So too did grow the
>Circle Of Purple
>a purple bar,
>*en baston*.

The Haggard Woman *glances up from the book she's been reading & surveys her newfound surroundings...*

The wooden, word-burned tome is atop a two-wheeled pushcart placed in the epicentre of the circular room. 'Tis the centrepiece, & the only 'true' furniture, in the chamber.

Twenty-one clear-glass ◊-windows ~ paned high up in the brickwork walls, spaced out in sets of threes ~ leam Disc-light into the near-hollow ringroom.

The hag eyes the wrought-grille ~ portcullis in design ~ overlaid upon the wooden slab door. The portway, horseshoe in shape, is arched o'er arriere-voussure. Artsy, not defensive architecture, she concludes, noting no bolt to lock the passageway up.

Hearthless, barren of the usual articles of a domicile, she ponders on this entrance halls' function. Skirting the curving walls, save near-abouts the doorway, is a built-in 'bench' or 'couch' along the circumference of the room, padded with a mosaic of pincushion pillows. 'Tis a writing & recitation room, she decides.

She eyeviews up at the wood beam ceiling. Surely, there's an upperfloor! Yet, no stairwell, ladder or floor door appear within her sight.

Glancing down to the undercarriage of the bookcarte, she scopes the implementia used to word-burn the book, stored in a chestbox.

Suspicion ~ *the kind that o'ercomes someone convinced not everyothing greeting the eye is always what it appears to be* ~ gets the hag's curiosity humming.

Hmmm ~ she wonders, stepping away from the book & waltzing 'round the curvature of the winding wall ~ *there's got to be an upper-room & a way to get there!*

Aha! Clever little builder ~ art thou!

She discovers a stairway concealed in the masonry of the doorway's archwork. Ascending the steep steps, the hag reaches the landing & realizes each half-arch supports an updown & downup stairwell. *'Tisn't 'hidden' for the sake of deceit,* she resolves ~ *'twas built this way for practical purposes: doesn't disrupt natural light nor take up unnecessary space.*

The hag brushes aside the beadstring curtain dangling from the portal at the top of the stairs & stares in: living quarters! She enters.

The only 'window-light' comes from a glass enclosed aperture in the centre of the ceiling ~ 'tis enough to Disc-beam in the awe of the dawe. The ceiling window is strange in design ~ a ☆-shape ne'er before seen nor read nor heard about by the hag!! For certain, she doesn't want to understand!!! Yet, for reasons unclear ~ e'en to herself ~ she walks o'er & stands directly underneath the pane.

The Disc dazzles its lux in streamers!!!

She *veils her eyes with her shawl & backs off from the sight!!! The Disc is a Disc ~ not a fiery flickering ball of flames like some word-burner's or blacksmith's bellows-fanned firepit!! 'Tis a trick of glass!!! 'Tis all it is.*

The Haggard Woman reels around as if to run & eyes herself in a mirrorstone, propped up on a selfsupporting stand. "Oh, my," she says aloud & to herself, "not bad for an old biddy!" She forgets the 'why' of her fright.

Regaining her composure, she reflects on the room in another light ~ this guy 'likes' to play tricks-on-the-iris! That's it.

She sees a sideboard table with a washbasin next to the strawstack bed & steps over to it. Splashing water onto her face, her thoughts drift off to the book downstairs...

'Circle Of Purple'? What nonsense. She's not heard such a history before!! What kind of word-burner is this strange man with such a strange roundhouse!?!

Patting her face dry with her shawl, the hag takes a closer examination of the 'upper-loft'. Ambries are cupboarded into the walls where windows, she thinks, should be. Apart from the bed, the table & some wallhooks for clothes & a bunch of chest-trunks strewn about, not much up here, presumes she. Then she turns again to face the mirror ~ what's that behind it? A ladder leading to a trapdoor, eyes she.

Looking *out from behind the crenels & merlons of the rooftop of the roundhouse, the hag eyes The Windy Way, from which she came earlier in the day, & observes something odd! She o'erviews a peculiarity o'erlooked on the walk: the two-rut lane of The Windy Way rolls upto the doorway of this house. She runs over to the other side of the turret & sees the road continuing alongside the house as a footpath.*

The old woman races o'er to the opposite side of the roof ~ sure as can be, The Windy Way is no longer cartwheel rutted, 'tis as singlefile as any game trail!!!

Turning about she catches a glimpse of another sight ~ on a near distant hillslope she can see the CIRCLE OF PURPLE!!! ~ PURPLE BAR EN BASTON & all!!!!!

Stunned as if stung by a bumblebird, she knows not what to think. She eyes it again & there it be. ' & yes ~ it has always been.'

The Haggard Woman hears a shout & off in the distance comes awalking The Rainbow Man a-waving & another. On closer approach she footnotes: The Brun Girl.

Naw, thinks the hag, she's too veal-side, not enough on the heifer-half for his likenings ~ as she waves down.

Feeling like a stray houseguest, she retracks down the ladder & stairs to the front of the strange roundhouse & waits outside.

14
THE
LOST
SUPPER

Low the blow
Laid by the thief
Who strikes
In the good-gloom
Of dinnertime.
Brief be thy tenure
Of time
Before ye repent
Of thy crime!

Fictionairy

<u>Mellisonant</u> < sweet smelling, as rare fresh air or the vague remembrance of such a nonthing
<u>Escriteau</u> < a menu guide for the food preparer as compared to a bill of fare for table guests
   ✝ for further reference on the above noun, the publisher suggests the following authoritative works, *if still in print:*
   Le Maître d´ hôtel français
       2 volumes
   Le Pâtissier royal parisien
       2 volumes
   Le Cuisinier parisien
   L´ Art de la cuisine au dix-neuvième siècle
       5 volumes
   Le Pâtissier pittoresque
all the above ✝✝✝✝✝ by Marie-Antoine Carême
(b. 1784 - 1833 d.) who signed his works by dropping the Marie
<u>Tranchoirs</u> < erstwhile clever way of using up stale bread, replaced for a time by inedible wooden planks until plattery came into vogue

As the foot sounds & chitchat of The Rainbow Man & The Brun Girl wind-blow nearer, The Haggard Woman readjusts her shawl & grabbles for her cowlstaff. The hag hobbles o'er to a hedge & listens to the aria hymn of a birdcall. Thinks she: such sweet sounds abound in the backyard of Fornia, far from the clothlines & other flimsy boundary posts betwixt the close-packed cottages of De Vow Lay. She takes in a whiffsniff of country air & wishes if only her life's breath could be inspired in such an idyllic sweetsmelling spot. She takes in mellisonant thoughts & soughs to the croon of the breeze.

The Brun Girl rounds the roundhouse & smiles to the hag. "Howya do'n there?" asks she.

"Fine & dandy-o," responds the hag & adds "how's about you?"

Before the lass can reply, The Rainbow Man comes arunning holding his nose with his hands & heads for the other side of the hedge.

"Aaaaaaaaaaaaah! A$^a{}_a{}^a$h$_h$h cc^{h}h$_{hooooOO}$!!" is heared from the unseen hedgeside.

"Don't mind him none," states The Brun Girl with an air of acquaintancy, "*he* always has to go sneeze around these parts ~ must be some unseeable thing in the ether, or something."

The Rainbow Man ~ always showing allergic symptoms by the simplest of things ~ looks down to the ground in disgust!

His wheazy sneeze has begotten an *ughly!!!* green snotslug. 'Tis almost an unnameable life form. Thank the nature of things, the man exclaims to himself ~ anyothing that slimy does not deserve to live in any epoch!! Thankfully, the substance is exuded stillborn.

Noticing the mucous honey-spotches on his sleeve, The Rainbow Man yanks off his shirt & kicks it o'er into some dirt. Unhappy with its shoddy burial, the man tears it into shreds & tosses it into a nearby unlit firepit ~ his outside hearth, no doubt. He also hides it under some charcoals. For good measure, he then covers the briquettes with ash.

Methodical in his bizarre goingsabout, the man returns to the scene of the snotslug & buries the booger under a fist-size rock.

The fibrous hyphae of the local fungus clump immediately thank the overlords & miladies of the undersoils for the miraculous spoils & make plans to share it with the finest, hairlike rootlets of the nearby ne'ergreen tree, in exchange for sugar, of course!

The top-naked man steps 'round the bushes ~ his torse smeared with the smudge of soot ~ & doffs his floppy hat as he bypasses the ladies & disappears into his house.

What the jibberjabbberwhat'sthematter!??? is written on the two femmens' faces as the man races by! They smirk & smile & laugh aloud ~ so wholeheartily The Haggard Woman unloosens her shroud.

The Brun Girl says nothing. Her eyes twinkle.

"You won't say a word to him, will ya?" The Haggard Woman asks, unshawling her head for the first, intentional, time. Shewn is shown.

"Not my prob," chirps The Brun Girl.

"Known him long?" inquires Shewn.

"Who?" answers the girl with an askance.

"The Rainbow Man?"

"Oh, you mean *The Professor.* Yea, & naw ~ he's not one to let ya get to know him. Guess you could say he's unknowable," responds The Brun Girl fidgeting with her brun hair curls.

Shewn *aka* The Haggard Woman hmmms ~ this lil, not so *little*, lassy here, ain't exactly the game winner of brains. She spouts out, "Didn't you call 'im *Zipfly* earlier today?" She asks the question not really expecting a straightforward answer.

"Heh," The Brun Girl retorts as if straining her memory bank, "I dunno ~ *maybe.* I call *all* the guys that ~ I think. What you know about him anyoway? Where'd ya meet him?" The girl asks more out of smalltalk than big thoughts.

"To tell ya the truth," states The Haggard Woman *aka* Shewn, "this midmorn I *almost* believed he was trying to get into my britches in a woodstock!"

"Him, naw ~ he's not *that* way," The Brun Girl flatly relates as tho if her curves didn't work, *who's* would.

"What way?"

"Ah, ya know, he's got his head stuck in his book, that's all."

"You e'er read in it?" asks the woman.

"Read? *Who* me? No way," the girl states & goes on, "he reads to us, sometimes, when he has a mind to & when he's around ~ he's always off somewhere, it seems. Even when he's around."

Shewn hears the door opening & reverts back into The Haggard Woman ~ wrapping her face in her headshawl.

The Rainbow Man comes out of the house hatless, donning a blouse & wearing a smile. He seems a *changed* man. "Ladies, 'tis your lucky good-gloom! Tonight I'm going to prepare us a feast worthy of the greatest pigfest of the best great hall!!" he boasts.

The Haggard Woman, unaccustomed to the local protocol, wonders *where's* he going to get, fix & dish up these vittles.

"Goodygooodygooooodie," gigglegoos The Brun Girl, hopping like she's got to go do what the nature of things calls on all to do. "I gotta go take care of *whizzybiz"* she throws in, making it a public announcement.

"Yea, why don't you go do that," the man says looking towards The Windy Way, "& why don't you show The Haggard Woman the way, too."

The Haggard Woman hppps at this! Dang know-it-all ain't he!? ~ thinks the hag as she follows The Brun Girl 'round the hedgerow & finds to her surprise a maze of bushy passage ways past the outdoor hearth & dining room.

"Wow!" The Brun Girls blurbs out, "did ya see all those fresh mushstumps, back there?"

"No where?"

"When we first 'round the 'corner' ~ I'll bet he's going to fix'n up something with 'em."

Shewn *feels* like a haggard woman around this young bloomflower headpuff.

The cracking aroma of vine trimmings & sparks of allnut shells & charks of ambrosial tree bark charcoal their harmonious medley o' well chosen fuels ~ sniffs The Haggard Woman, versed-well in the arts of cookery smells.

Howtheheckinbrazes does he do it? simmers the hag: *we* weren't gone but a few moments!!

The Rainbow Man perches on a rock-chair athroned in a chefdom of squalid splendor. On a nearby flatrock griddle, ironed in among the coals, a dozen or more mummingbird eggs are a-sizzling along with wild herbs bowtied in clumps & crybaby onions cradled in nests of baby turnips, parsnips & beets ~ held together with the straws of coarse, allgrain bread. O'er the firepit, a well-basted ribeye roast of furry-tail rests upon a spit. Dangling down from the makeshift rôtisserie, a hollow'd-out gourd wafts wisps of steeping rabbitroot & other teas.

Mymy ~ hungrycat eyes The Haggard Woman at the sight of the culinary orgy.

"To eat alone is social onanism," the man says slyly to his bystanding company, "come & sit & enjoy."

"What's *On & Iz Em?*" The Brun Girl asks in puzzlement taking a stone seat at the far end of the firepit.

"A term *only* a master baker would know," The Haggard Woman answers up wryly, giving the man a glom.

Touché, The Rainbow Man thinks glancing up at The Haggard Woman. "Methinks you may not have any teeth, hag, but you do know how to read, don't you?" he queries.

"Teeth enough to jawgash you," says she teasingly.

The Brun Girl thinks *maybe* she should leave, or something, as she eyes these two, one, then the other. Hmmm ~ they're speaking in a language of *only* two ~ wormholes she.

She needn't despair...

A horse is heard galloping up to the front of the roundhouse & slowing to a stop.

"We're back here!" half-shouts The Rainbow Man to the unseen rider. "Brought something more stalwart than weed-flavoured water, me hopes," he wishbones in words.

"Dangdern, Cheffrey, one can smack at your savory trail from here to the next pisshole!" taunts a voice beyonder the hedge.

The Haggard Woman listens to the sounds of dismounting & spurred footsteps coming anigh as The Rainbow Man prods the flames with a poker & sparkfairies dance aloft the meal.

A green-bottle is hurled o'er the hedge; The Rainbow Man catches it with his dexter hand ~ seemingly not e'en looking up. More sparks fly.

"Got cups?" the late arriver asks.

"Yea, & your dangdern pottle is a-leaking!"

"Ya said ya didn't want *water!*"

The faceless voice takes bodily form.

The Haggard Woman stares at the big, burly red-haired man. He's trousered & bloused & high-top booted. A slouchy hat half covers one side of his head.

"Greetings, Sire, mihag, my lil juicesqueeze, scooch o'er, hon," the man says to The Brun Girl.

She does, not showing much interest. Outwardly anyway.

"Welcome, Sire Woodright. I thought you said you'd come tomorrow?" vocals the host.

The Haggard Woman didn't recognize the man without his coat-of-rust. Hmmm ~ thinks she, appearances are all too easily misleading, like, like *me!! I wonder what they think of me?* ~ a hag, no doubt & 'tis my fault!!!

"What is a tomorrow?" Woodright asks. Then answers, "A tomorrow is a wishful period of time promised to none of us. We only have what we have ~ *this* dawe called today."

"Well put," says The Rainbow Man beginning to place the wellfixed fare of the escriteau upon tranchoirs...

Some things happen within a span of time & a split of space so fast as to make the chestpump race! A knight agleaming in armor shiny onrushes past on a fullspurred charger & with him ~ the main course of the repast!! 'Twas lancer-lotted in a *flash!!!*

Woodright jumps to his heels & grasps the tail wind of the gush with his mighty fist. *Swishh!* is all he catches.

The Haggard Woman hops up from her tailend piece & scotches on her feet in a feat worthy of a circus performer! The sound of *something!* releases from her windpipe. A sound no word-burned inscription can relate with any precision ~ an onomatopoeia of *surprise!* is the best & only way to describe the shriek!!!

The Brun Girl dives into the hedge-thickets like a pluckpluck ~ feather strowing, not e'en knowing where her head is going!

The Rainbow Man, coop-robbed of the *piece d' resistance,* goes about doing the remainder of his job ~ he dishes up the eggs & onions & tea & such, without so much as a shrug.

"Sit & eat," is all he says, without a pother of preparing himself a platter ~ after an added *"please!"*

The three guests sit down, after a matter of some time, as The Rainbow Man gets up, excusing himself, "Pardon me, I have to write."

Walking away he says over his shoulder, "Do not fret, he won't be back ~ this eve."

The Haggard Woman, tired of pretense, takes off her shawl & throws it into the firepit ~ the sparkle fairies fly high above the spangling, glow-cooling coals.

The threesome eyes the pixies' flight.

A long stint of silence follows before the trio returns to the realm of words. 'Tis helped alot by the contents of the passaround green-glass bottle.

"Names, not noms, please & truth-of-pasts," beseeches the knight ~ the first affected by the fiery water. He confesses, "I, I'm ~ hmmm ~ *Kcirtap, the Third*, I think. My family's been decastled since my father's pa's da's Sire."

"I'm *Shewn*," the woman publicizes, "jus' a reader in search of a writer. I, I hail from the nearabouts of El Lay. I'm also a mom ~ of an MCB ~ presently unwedknotted."

The girl speaks up, "Hiya all, my name is *Liz* & my *mom* is Lady Lord Mayor of El Lay ~ & she's a guzzleress, a liaress & the loosest legs e'er met ~ that's why I had to get away. How ~ *how* could I e'er be expected to live up to her reputation & expectations?   She is considered *great!!!*" The Brun Girl starts to pout in tears, eyewater tracks her cheeks.

"Now, now, child," pampers Kcirtap, "may I escort you back to your home tonight?"

"No, take me to your place," says she.

"What about Shewn?" he asks the both.

"Shewn will be fine, right here," asserts the woman taking pity on the girl. "Take her ~ be off, go on, get going."

The last flares of the firepit sparkle as the night rises & the knight & damsel ride off.

15
CEREMENT ON THE MOUNT

Wrapped within
The burial shroud,
Peabrainless stuff
Waxen cerecloth'd,
Is allowed
To be disendowed.
The ceremony
Takes place
Without a word
Spoken aloud.

Fictionairy

<u>Cerement</u> < 1. clothes one, or something, is buried in 2. same as cerecloth: a burial cloth
<u>Cerecloth'd</u> < ✝ past tense of above (!?!)
<u>Skiffing</u> < navigating without aid or sense of course or direction (???)
<u>Misplaced comma</u> < meaning, &, origin, not, clear,
<u>Persiflage</u> < raillery
<u>Thrave</u> < 1. formerly a measure of 24 sheaves of wheat 2. now: two dozen anyothing
<u>Sherds</u> < same as shards
<u>Scaurs</u> < same as sherds
<u>Sharding</u> < the makings of scaurs
<u>Orthography</u> < 1. correctly spelling words 2. wordspelling correctly 3. word perfect-ism in the inexactness of persiflage
<u>Oscitancy</u> < 1. yawnfully 2. *& Indifference*

Nightrise looms up fast & Shewn seeks haven from the gloam as the embers of the firepit choke on their last puffs of barbeque-breath smoke. Gelid clouds of the shroud of night are as thick as brickwalls & she stumbles her way into the hedge before skiffing 'round the thicket fence. Playing a solitaire hand of blindgirlbluff she blumbles & flubs until she slams into the roundhouse door. Dithering on whether or not to knock & announce her ingression, she stalls, pausing like a misplaced comma. *What's he going to do ~ say 'skitskat-skiddoo'!?* Rethinking ~ *did he not offer his house this day? Yea, to The Haggard Woman, not to Shewn! Nay, I do not swallow 'tis his wont to turn anyone away!* Shivering, she throws off all this selfsuggesting hollowheaded persiflage & barges in.

The room is aglow with the flickering tongues of no less than thrave candleflames propped on chest-trunks strewn about centrestage of the circular room. An eerier glowth emits from one metallic trunk nearer the bookcarte, at the feet of the man hunchbacking o'er his word-burning a-smoulderings.

"Methought I harkened voices outside," says The Rainbow Man not looking o'er his shoulder.

"Ye harkened only methoughts inside," voices the woman.

"What's that ya say?" catechizes he, like a haggard man, handcupping an ear as an aid in hearing.

"I said," Shewn makes up, "'tis as smoky in here as it is shroudy outside."

The man picks up a woodburning tidbit tool, tip & all, & lobs it thru one of the ◊ windows. The glass shatters into sherds & the scaurs of broken pane shower down ~ mostly sharding the outside ground. He tosses another, missing the mark & the point. The awl-like implement dart-sticks into a ceiling beam & twangs like a bowstring before releasing its untenable hold. It stabs a pincushion with a *pfffph.* He grabs a bottle from the undercarriage of the cart...

"THAT'S ENOUGH!" shouts Shewn at the top of her vocal range.

The whoop is loud enough for the man to be taken aback & take ahold of himself.

Shewn feels the man's word-burning eyes sear into her unmasked face. Says she to break his piercing glaze, "I apologize for shouting. Ummm ~ 'tisn't imperative for you to break your tools which are essential for your writing, you know. If you want, I'll open up the door to get some ventilation in here for ya." She heads for the entrance & then stops midway. Eye-turning towards the man, she asks, "Are you going to throw that bottle, too?"

"Why not, 'tis empty of penblood, anyway," sasses he with an air of insouciance. "A poet without penblood ~ what good is he? Good for nothing," he asks & answers, glancing now at the bottle in his hands.

"Penblood?!" backtalks Shewn. *"Penblood* has got to be the most, the *most!,* superfluous peabrainless part of so-called ~ uncalled for ~ handuscripting that I've e'er heard of!!! What need of paint has word-burning? None, laddy-o. 'Tis as peacockish, as pavo cocky, as a cock on a peahen!!! What need has a layhen of a set of peanuts?! Why strut what needn't be fantailed? 'Tis the dodoest, oofbirdieish, bird-dumbest thing in the world!!!"

"As peafowlish as orthography?" the man interrupts, showing sure signs of oscitancy.

"I wouldn't go quite that far!"

"How 'bout as asinine as a comely woman shawling 'hind the scowl of an old hag?"

Good repartee to you, thinks she. "Look, 'tis late & you've made a mess of your place. Let me help you clean it up ~ it seems to me that you're done with writing for the night."

"Done, done, yes I'm done ~ the *book* is done," the man announces, still holding onto the penblood-dry bottle.

"Is it done, *it is,* now!!?!!" Shewn exclaims more than erotemes.

"Quite so," The Rainbow Man yawns out, taking the rainbow coloured scarf off his neck & wrapping the bottle with it.

Shewn's eyes follow the man's actions, not quite sure what they're leading to, or why.

As he blows out the candles, one at a time, he lets the teardrops of tallow dripple onto the scarf-enfolded decanter. Continuing this odd *ritual* ~ such as it is ~ until only two candles remain lit, the man seems pleased with his waxy-clothed mummy-jar & sets it aside. Picking up the next-to-the-last candle, he sleepily sways o'er to the nearest to him part of the pincushioned bench, & flops himself down as if hitting the hay. Blowing out the candle, says he, "Know the way to the upstairs, don't ya?"

"Yes," Shewn replies to the dark.

"You really think penblood is unnecessary?" the man in the dark asks.

"Yes," says Shewn picking up *her* candle & flickering her way towards the stairwell.

The dark asks, "What's your name?"
"Shewn," the walking candle answers.
The candle inquires, flickering, "& yours?"
"The Rainbow Man," replies the dark.
"See you in the dawnfall," the candle-halo bids.
The dark doesn't answer.
The candle glows away.

Shewn wakes early. Hmmm ~ thinks she, first dawe she hasn't felt haggard since she left home. *Home* ~ her mind wanders to her MCB, her cottage, her life in De Vow Lay. Seems close, e'en the afar flowers in her garden. Tho afar, the things held in the heart are always anear, smiles she.

Lifting her head up, Shewn notices herself, rather her reflection, in the mirrorstone & says "You need a hairwash, milady!"

Wait a moment comes a thought amiss. The mirrorstone, it wasn't *there* yesterday ~ 'twas o'er there! She sits up on the strawbed & eyes the ☆ ceiling window. 'Tis covered over from the outside, *by what?* A thin blanket, she surmises. Another surprise greets her on the side table: juice, fruits, breads & jam! Standing up, Shewn takes in other amenities: lemon flowers in the washbasin, a towel folded neatly o'er & topped with a rose bud. Perhaps, it isn't as early as methinks ~ thinks she.

Shewn performs her ablutions, snacks a bite, downs a quaff & hops more than steps downstairs. The Rainbow Man isn't there. After appraising the changes in the room at a quick glance ~ the chest-trunks are closed & stacked next to the bookcarte, all-in-all, most of the mess of the night before beseems tidied up somewhat ~ Shewn runs outside & hollers, "Hello!"

Only a bullfrop belches back a *gjuuruurp*.

Dashing back inside, she scrambles up the stairs, escalades the ladder & peers out o'er the parapet. Eye-scouring the countryside, The Rainbow Man is seen: atop the crest of a hill ~ the Circle Of Purple mount.

"Hey, there!" the man hears as he turns to see the seamstress breeze pinning her dress in tight-fitting ripples. Femman features endure a more than modest grazing by the man's eyes. Her blon hair blows & bows in curly tresses, pressed up, down & around by the wind's caresses.

"Where've you been?" asks the *'Hey, there!'*
"Oh, out & about, burying some peabrainless stuff," comes the reply.
"There are better things to do than that."
"Like wha..."
The voices begin osculating & the two figures meld into the poppy-blanketed hillside.

16
QUEAN
OF THE
OBLONG VALLEY

Quean is the misruler
Of The Oblong Valley.
None could be crueler
Than this back-alley
Vamp gone bigwig!
Till came a tramp ~
Her unrelenting dueler ~
Whose thingumajig
It was to ridicule her!

Fictionairy

Cinct < to be surrounded by; encircled
Divellicated < put asunder
Victrix < a femman victor
Enceinte < the curtain wall of a castle; specifically, the outerworks of the fortress strong
Baileys < 1. courtyards enclosed by enceinte 2. a refreshing beverage in civilized & holy londes
Meurtières < arrow-loop windows, also called 'murder holes' by some, mostly dead
Mesnie < the armed &/or armored personnel of a castle household, as compared to halfmen or chambermaids, etc.
Picayune < smallfry
Doss < a cheap bed, as in a flophouse
Lopjobbed < past tense of lopjob: circumcision of the head
Ruction < the eruption of Celtic clans and the like, coming together ~ or something similar
Coffle < something awful, like being chained in a gang

Quean of The Oblong Valley was never-never a Princess. Howbeit, once she was Queen of all Fornia ~ thru connubiality with The King. The King was not only heretofore a Prince, but also *the* Heir by birth, default & defect. He became King by the deathwish of the deathbedridden Ol' King Calidad ~ the wishbone of his older bro, the late Duke of De Citi ~ who did not want to be The King & never-never was ~ & by the deadhead misdeeds of his younger bub, Calilad ~ whose wishfulness to be *anything* at all will never-never be fulfilled. When The King unwedknotted his bedded Queen, for reasons unclear, she became a Quean by profession.

The King, for clear-cut reasons, sequesters his Kingsly selfsame in Ashameaway Castle, a place where no roads lead to or fro, cinct by a lakeshore moat, approachable only by barge or boat ~ if e'er anyoyou want to go.

Thusly, the Kingship of our land slinks away, becoming a more than less impotent position. It isn't e'en important to the last remaining relics of the Upmost Ruling House of Royalty. Hmmm ~ like *what's-her-name?,* Lady Lord Mayor of El Lay ~ who, by the way, really does have a road leading into The Oblong Valley! Surely, the moo-cow isn't any otherhow divers than t'other pignoblefemman.

Anyoway, Quean, whose given or liven name is Mari Posa, divellicated by her Sire, was castoff into The Oblong Valley ~ the lowliest of lowly places on the face of Fornia.

There, she excelled her antecedent Queenly role by rolling in the haystacks. Needless to say, she became exceptionally successful.

A victrix in the clover ~ rarer moreover than success in private commerce ~ is always more gainful than the hohum rollover of Ascendancy in the Royal bedchamber.

Mari Posa, with her hindmost-begotten gains built herself a selfname castle nearabouts no Walled In Town, dungeon, dunghole, village, croft or hovel.

Albeit, success stories are seldom 'e'erafter'.

Flutterbys are Quean's wheal, not her slapside as many may imagine.

Her castle is built like no other. 'Tisn't e'en a castle in the classical sense. Its lofty square keep isn't protected nor connected by enceinte. Quean has no need for any, nor for baileys. What she wants & needs flies in daily & nets are the make of her worth.

No meurtières sneer out their sinister slitty leers from Mari Posa Castle. Great breezeway ◻-apertures, alit nightrise to dawnfall, beckon & beacon another malign design: to attract as many flutterbys & colourflies as can be drawn in. These fairylike flitters on the whimsical wing aren't as bright as one might think. Light lures these dimwitty critters.

No need has Quean for hobnoggin things like villages & tillages. The scaly wings of the lepidopts is what she pillages. In truth, fluthe ~ the fabric made of the waxy wings ~ is the most lucrative & coveted cloth in the grabrag trade. Quean, of course, corners the market.

Quean may be a painted lady, but she is no dodobimbodumbeedo!

Bear with the word-burner: Quean may be as bald as an auld tortoise head ~ 'tis e'en said her fuzzless noggin is as sheen as a bean & no grass is felt tween her hills & dales, so trodden is the o'erworn path ~ yet e'en a lady so tainted can be a thinker.

Now, her nonclassy castle is not indefensible! Nay, this drossel is verily sensible. Hindsight is wizdom only *if* arses have eyeballs & Quean is in the bizdom of aforethought.

The aegis of Quean's fluthe market & her castle is based upon her mesnie of dread ~ her arm of harm, the filth of illth, namely, The Unred Knights.

Not knights are they as in the chivalrous glory of knighthood's heydawe. Knight dejects are the mainstay of this rejected sect.

They aren't knights in rusty suits of battered iron, a-mount on trustworthy steeds ~ not this breed.

Quean's brand of knights are the prissy-sissy spangle-shiny medal-bearers who ne'er fair-ye-fight & who delight in their dastardly service as steady paidmen!

Calilad ~ whose kinship holds the Kingship of Fornia, such as it is ~ calls himself, no jest, *The Marshalissimo!* & leader of this brigade of brigands!! Altho, e'en his so-called vassals at Mari Posa Castle refer to him as Mari's lil lad ~ & other shoefits-wear-its. Even an Unred can tell the difference twixt a picayune clog & a bigwig gizmo!!!

Under the armpits of this cavalry of evilry, an infantry of bowmen & foemen & lowmen trample. 'Tis the vilest horde that e'er was overlorded by a Quean of Whoredom-come.

Precious as the stuff called fluthe may be ~ especially so to those who grow what others sew ~ those who are impressed into the servitude of servicing this trade are made into chattel!

Treated worse than cattle, are they!!

Peeons Quean calls 'em, if anything at all!

Burlap sack is *their* only clotheswrap.

Unsalable midsections of the flutterbys are *their* only allotment of nutrition!

Quean doesn't e'en let these downtrodden, miserable wretches pitch *their* squalid huts within sight of her castle or eyeview.

Thus, they must walk long stretches to & fro *their* arduous labours!

Why do they do it? 'Tisn't because these folksy denizens of The Oblong Valley want to be amicable neighbors! 'Tis simply that there isn't a choice.

Encroachers & poachers are brought back to the castle & turned into Quean's servant *boys.* Those who dither at her come-hithers don't get a stab at secondchance! From laundry lads to garderobe attendants, stable stewards to Great Hall garçons ~ allmen become halfmen for spurning her dally! Effeminated gelds, neuters unfit as suitors, caponed they are upon her dais for not tossing in her doss.

Worse is the loss to runaway *peeons!* If caught they're lopjobbed on the spot, headfirst.

Hear ye now how one dawe, a stranger traipsed into the valley & came upon a hobbledehoy. "Boy," saith the outlander, "let us hobnob."

The lad was sore afraid of a lopjob & sayeth he was taught not to talk to strangers.

The outlander saith "I hold no danger for thee; let us walk, then," & handed him a wineskin to partake from & drench his quench.

The lad blenched & refused to clench the proffered botabag.

Saith the outlander, "Within this wineskin is mulse & krasis ~ teatotally inferior for a ferment drink ~ look ye at the exterior: 'tis a sketch of a route thru the fog-bearded hills. Stretcheth & etcheth the sack ~ it shall be made clear."

The stranger tossed the winebag to the lad & bade him, "Few are the dawes left to thee."

"What is thy name & what art thou about?" asks the lad.

"What I am about is written. My name is not one to be remembered. How art thou called?" questions the stranger.

"Ob Tamota."

"Saq is how ye shall be known. Be off & take thy people to safety."

"But, *they* will murther us if we go."

"They know not what they are doing ~ go now in one piece!" bade the outlander, "Few are the dawes ~ time runneth!"

Strange things began to befall The Oblong Valley. Nightrise would find trees trimmed into the shapes of birds, scarecrows to flutterbys. Dawnfall: squalid huts pitched within view of Quean & every aperture of Mari Posa Castle, devoid of their builder(s).

Quean went froth at the mouthing!

Her Unreds hacked down every bird-trimmed tree & pyred each eyesore hutch. 'Tis all they could do, they couldn't catch the culprit(s)!

Her slash & burn tactics were becoming her ruin.

Flutterbys avoided the bonfire smoke & the derooted trees ~ even her tower!!!

Quean suspected many treacheries. Especially so, when the last peachtree was chopped down & the mutilator was yet to be found!!!!

Her tirades became the daily rage!!!!!

Calilad, Unreds, allmen, lowmen, halfmen cowered & kowtowed to their frothing Quean, powerless it seemed, to stop the rut-buildings & tree debauchery!

Fluthe production took a plunge as flutterbys avoided her rook.

Came the dawe, *peeons* didn't e'en come.

"They shan't go in one piece!" avowed Quean rallying up her entourage.

Calilad pointed to a not so far off hillside & asked "Who is *that* fluxfluthen man?"

"Harass *that* man!" ordered Quean.

Shewn looks up from The Book after flipflopp'n o'er several blank plank leafs. Hmmm ~ so the Bicch *did* get around to eating up his woodburn' illustrations, afteritall ~ o well.

Jus' then, the door bursts open & an onrush of 'vistors' gushes in. "Mom!" & "Shewnee!" & e'en a *meoow* is overheard from the ruction!!!

She eyes the MCB, Granny, & the Question Mark Cat with newfound kittymate in the ruckus as a raven swoops in.

"Mom," reports the MCB, "it was awful! We came look'n for ya & the Unreds caught us & The Windy Wayfarers & chained us in a coffle! The *Quean* is coming after The Bookman!!"

Shewn asks The Rainbow Man, whom her son is fingering, "Who are all these *other* people?"

The Bonedry Clan from beyon' The Impassable are introduced, as are the Crowkeepers & Saq & his band of Oblongers. The Windy Wayfarers exchange greetings with the locals & t'others.

The Rainbow Man explains "Calilad followed me from The Oblong Valley. Quean rounded up these hostages & exchanged them for The Book ~ she doesn't like the contents, you could say. Anyoway, I lied. I can't & shan't turn The Book over to her."

"No," reaffirms Shewn hugging her MCB, "a promise made to a kidnapping hussy is not a vow, anyohow. Is there a game plan?" asks she, as cat-whiskers nudge her knee.

17
BATTLE
IN THE
COW PATTIES

Tho leg or arm be broken
From the battle
None came back dead.
Lo! The Rainbow Man fell
& many hearts bled.
'Twas said: He'll be back
To tell his tales.
Wails from the ditch
Told of a fate
Worse than the Bicch!

Fictionairy

<u>Tintamarre</u> < a nightmare of noise, even in the light of unsleepy-eyed dawe

<u>Drapeaus</u> < drapery, *pl.* as in those laid over the shoulders of pages, trumpeteers & other stick people; under saddles, etc.

<u>Ataxian</u> < 1. an eerie feeling that wormholes into one's noggin when *things* are not happening in a normal manner 2. worm-churnings in one's gut 3. confusion 4. a misuse of ataxia 5. a cab driver a-metering

<u>Great Silvery Bird</u> ~ *with eyes on its side!* < Singasling Airways Flight 86

<u>Targe</u> < 1. a thing a coward uses always & a brave one not oft enough; also called a *shield* 2. *v.t.* to keep under discipline 3. badmouthing

<u>Barb & Vire</u> < the frontis & tailpiece of an arrow

<u>Neb-flies</u> < a metaphor for flying sharp pointed things, usually made by stick people for eyeing the noggins of others

<u>Remeant</u> < past tense of *v.i.* 'to return or go back' ~ never-never in common usage

<u>Real Manly Man</u> < long-form for RMM

Came dawn & all aves spring aloft taken on one wing of flight. Forthwith comes the lapin & their next of hopalong kin, followed by, then overtaken by, hoofing herds of buck, doe, roe & fawn ~ flushing from the brush as afore the rush of a firestorm. Behind the fauna the foe emerges thru the flora & enters upon the open playing field of wardom's ageold game of huff & bluff. Horns howl. Drumrolls rumble. Incessant winds subjoin the rattle of arms & armor, foot & saddle into a tintamarre of metal, carnal & leather clamor. Drapeaus flit. Pennons flutter the ritualized glamour of ataxian pageantry.

Those auditioning their bit parts gulp in silence as the choreographers of the sword-dance eye the marrowbone stage. Quean amends a few last moment step-by-step movements waltzing thru her a-boggling noggin.

Saq eyes his band of women, children & men as they huddle upon the little hill horn. Only Sire Woodright ~ Kcirtap ~ is armed, armored & a-mount, complete with raven aplume on his rusted crest. Saq turns his head & scams over to The Rainbow Man. *Dangdern, that one ~ he thinks ~ makes me 'leader' of this lost cause & all he does to advise me is tell me how & where to digdigdig & dig!!!*

Shewn bosom-holds the Question Mark Cat & scritches her cat-ears as the MCB pets daisy-lion a-purring. Granny & the Crowkeepers hold hands. The Brun Girl, Oxman, the Bonedry Clan & The Windy Wayfarers & Saq's little lot of Oblongers crouch upon the knoll awaiting the pending onslaughter, minding their time.

Shewn glances over at The Rainbow Man axle greasing his bookcarte. He turns & winks. Says he, "Saq, your people got two & a half man-size flutterby net poles, *right?* Have them raise 'em, please."

"Poles, erect!"

"Oxman," asks The Rainbow Man "how's your bullwacker?"

SssssswwaaaakK!!! goes the whip.

A terrible *shshriek!!* suddenly looms & booms, quaking the battleground with unheard before sounds. Both sides gaze up to the sign in the sky & awe a great silvery bird ~ *with eyes on its side!!!!*

"*For Forniiiiah!*" Woodright shouts spurring on his charger & galloping headlong to joust with the oncoming Unred demon zooming o'er his foemen's heads ~ flying without a wingflap, beelining straight towards the knoll.

Kaw kaw kowtow kowtow!!! caws the raven flapping up to intercept the intruder.

Across the line of battle, Calilad fidgets as if to flee from the onrushing challenge of the solo charging Red knight.

Quean grabs *The Marshalissimo's* bridlestrap, hoarse-shouting, "Do not embarass me in front of all these people! Hold your position!!"

The shiny big bird passes in a flash, far too high & fast for even the upswooping raven to get a talon dash at it. The tail of the giant dragonbug thing on a wing swiiishes a fleeting hole thru the rouge & blush fleece of the nebbia ~ revealing a glimpse of blueth!!!

Woodright U-turns his mount & trots back to the little hill to the cheers of his people & the jeers of Quean's menacing host as the raven returns to its shouldery roost.

The spectacle in the sky fades from the minds of the spectators, themselves all too soon to become participants in another exhibition much closer to the nittygritty.

Woodright rides in ~ nods to The Rainbow Man taking up a position in front of the lil hill with his bookcarte ~ & trots on, behind the knoll, without a word spoken.

"Drop your poles & take cover!" shouts Saq, almost as if reading from a cue-card.

The band of men, femmen & children take up their defensive postures, well-versed thespians enacting a dress rehearsal, they seem.

Across the intervening grassy terrain the force of intruding Horse & Foot pompom up a rallying show of esprit, hyping themselves into a frenzy ~ steel-nerving up for the finale.

"What do we want?"
"The BOOK!"
"What do we want??"
"THE BOOK!!"
"How we gonna get IT?"
"TAKE it!"
"How we gonna take IT?"
"Over THEIR rawbones!
OVER THEIR rawbones!!
OVER THEIR RAWBONES!!!"

The Rainbow Man, undaunted, reads...

'Tis here they disturb the pastures of cattle.
'Tis here they enter upon the field o' battle!
   Quean's armored column strides forth
      in cavalcade
   & vile cavalry display their chargers
      of war arrayed.
   A feign procession of evil horsemen
      on parade
   For the dust-kicking ménage is just
      a charade!
   For far behind & beyond the screen
   Infantrymen maneuvers hie unseen!!
Rows of footmen, each with broadshield
      & lance
Wedge into a phalanx to form the army's
      advance!!!
As twelve queues of archers with short-
      bow & quiver
Extend echelons from The Ledge-Edge to
      yonder river!!!!
A reserve body of men-at-arms of every
      description,
Impressed into military service en masse
      conscription ~
Tinkers & tailors unsuited for this kind o'
      employment ~
Stand nervously unsteady & edgy at their
      deployment.

Quean commands her troops leaning 'gainst
    a targe.
"Be ye knight, squire, swordman, or lance
    sarge ~
For the book, my bed!" Quean proffers at
    large!!
"Let arrows fly! Forward footmen! Knights
    charge!!!"

The Rainbow Man takes cover 'neath his bookcarte as swarms of razorsharp shafts descend upon the defenders. His two-wheeled trolley is pierced & nicked by the barb & vire volley of pricks & sticks. Miraculously the book escapes hits!!! Reappearing in a lull of the neb-flies he wheels the handcart to the dexter ~ riverside ~ flank & takes cover once more as arrows swoop 'round nearly point-blank in aim.

    Calilad averts his attentions from his flanking assault objective on the sinister side of the lil mound ~ & misobeys orders to encirc their rear ~ veering his sword & mounted wall of ironclads towards the man with the bookcarte. "Follow me where I go!" shouts he.

    The Rainbow Man instinctively rolls his wagon to the other side of the knoll ~ nearest The Ledge-Edge ~ with *The Marshalissimo!* & Co. deflecting again, pursuing in shiny suits!

    Calilad has *gotcha now!* echoing in his helm.

Now, Saq's position rests on a little horn hill
Where he & his band play only a defense drill.
The arrowy flocks of missiles are cleverly withstood
Under umbrellas of rawhides & shelters of soakwood!
Undeterred comes on the charge of Unred knighthood!
E'en the Δ of footmen is adeem to make it good!
Bowstrings ease their nocks & twangs & archeryhood.
Saq & The Bookman's reserve is thought merely Woodright
Or maybe ~ just maybe ~ peeons! with bogsod plows
When 'round the knoll comes a stampede of spooked cows!!!!
Quean's bowmen & reserves hightail it in lickety-splits
As the phalanx halts in place, bracing for the bovine blitz!!!!
Shield-to-shield, shoulder-to-shoulder a-pointing spears,
The wedge o' footmen await the bullfight of cows & steers!!!

Saq & Shewn & all the rest arise from their arrow-proof dugouts & taunt yelps & jeers as the attackers stop in their tracks! Woodright is all gettyup & go as he drives the hoof'n herd smack thru the formation.

> Hooves & hulk heave their bulk upon the tightknit body.
> As the dusty cloud settles down nothing stands unshoddy!
> Shields are dents & bent & a-twist like wrist-joints!!
> Spears are broomsticks & men plead for mercy points!!!

Shewn eyes o'er to The Rainbow Man, nearby The Ledge-Hedge ~ still reading his book!!! He glances up at her & smiles ~ or smirks. Dang-dern that man!! ~ thinks she ~ glad that he is unhurt.

> Worst off the riders, befallen worse than death!
> With sight of their fate the battle lost its breath!!
> Fronting The Ledge-Edge flank was a grass hidden trench!!!
> Well greased & deep dug, full of cow patty dung-stench!!!

> Neither a horse nor a rider were spared
> the foul drench!
> That day Saq became a Prince & Quean
> his scullery-wench.

Some of Saq's band, wielding the two & a half man size flutterby net poles, extract the wallowing Unreds from their besmeared fates ~ after accepting their oaths of parole. Calilad, who led the charge, is the last yanked out of the *yuck!* Saq lets Sire Woodright exact the terms upon the Unreds: horses, arms & armor are turned o'er to the Oblongers. "Go now in one piece & take baths!!" bades Kcirtap.

The relic of the phalanx, being fearful of the revenge of the victors, expect to become the victims of afterkill. Aftersmell 'tis more likely ~ beaten by a foe possessing neither weapons nor omens of woe, the battered regiment rolls over in laughter!! Vowing each & every one to become bards & poetize the tattle of the Battle in the Cow Patties, the former warriors dance off beginning their new careers as wandering minstrels.

Quean, found hiding in a tree, is offered a job by her erstwhile *peeon,* & accepts. "Jobs are hard to come-by for an X flutterby Quean," she rationalizes. "Call me Mari."

"Madame Posi, methinks," says Saq.

Shewn having spent the midmorn with Granny & the MCB delighting at the ceremonies ending the fighting, is surprised to notice 'Rainbow' still nose-diving in his book so long after the outcome. Hmmm ~ *what could he be doing at The Ledge-Edge! He knew the conclusion afore the beginning!* She waltzes o'er to the man.

"Why are you still o'er here?" asks she as the blowsome winds near The Ledge-Edge whip her skirt o'er her face. "Mymy, I forget how windy it is *here!*" says she, pulling down her garment.

The Rainbow Man doesn't answer, grimaces.

"What's wrong?! *Are you wounded??*" Shewn shrieks as she eyes his dilemma: The Rainbow Man *isn't* reading his book, now written, he *is* holding onto the bookcarte for dear-life!! *"Saq! Woodright! Somebody come quick!!!"*

The Rainbow Man starts to lose his grip on the cart & begins to slip o'er The Ledge-Edge into oblivion!!

"NO!" shouts Shewn as everybody runs over, pale faced at the sight!

"I'll be right back..." says he as his hat flies off & high, grasping the cart now with the grip of only one hand.

Woodright offers his lance. Saq, a flutterby net. Shewn, her hand. Oxman, his bullwhacker.

The rainbow man falls jus' as a blueth birdy something with enormous wings flits by.

Umpth ~ Shewn hears in her inner-ear as her heart flutters like a mummingbird wingflap. The others *hear* it too.

"Get back everyone!" Woodright forewarns as the bookcarte begins to tremble & teeters o'er ~ the wooden tome plops on a precarious craig of The Ledge-Edge.

"NO, no!" shouts Shewn o'er the windy blore "don't let The Book fall, too!"

The MCB crawls o'er to the tome, retrieving The Rainbow Man's last remaining remnant by pushshoving the weighty handuscript with his noggin. "Here ya go, mom," is all he says as the rescued book is scooched before her.

"I ne'er read that he, he, would leave me," sikes a haggard woman, talking softly.

"Now, now, dear, cheer up ~ there's plenty o' men for ya out there," states Granny flatly.

"Shut up, Granny!" commands the MCB.

"He said he'd be right back," pampers The Brun Girl in reassurance.

"Yes," says Woodright "he's always out & about on some journe or another. He'll return." As the crowd disperses upon their diverse destinies, Shewn asks Woodright "Who are those two up there upon the little hill horn?"

The rusty knight gazes up at the knoll & eyes the shadowy figures. "If I didn't know any better I'd say The King & the late Duke of De Citi," he states as the duo disappears into fog.

Saq returneth to the Oblong with his flock & swore to dismantle Mari Posa Castle & grow tomatoes. 'Twas said he took up archery.

Granny hobbled back to her shanty, along with the Bonedry Clan off to play in El Lay's waterworks.

The Crowkeepers remeant to their croft.

The Windy Wayfarers went about their ways.

Oxman built The Rainbow Man's tome another bookcarte & pushed it back to the roundhouse before he set out upon a long journe. "Ne'er know what I might learn!"

Woodright & The Brun Girl ne'er wedknotted but tarried about S'Kcirtap Castle ~ partially restoring its bygone glory & renaming it Eltsac S'Kcirtap. The raven was ne'er seen after the day of the Battle & ne'er a caw from it has since been heard.

Calilad is said to have gotten an egg-rotten job sous chefing in De Citi.

Shewn remained at the roundhouse with her MCB, the Question Mark Cat & the daisylion ~ the latter two-o learning well that nothing never changes.

The MCB, grown into a Real Manly Man, found himself centrestage of his generation.

Dawes faded away into bloomtimes & Shewn waited. Albeit, not for long.

18
CALIF
OF
FORNIA

Books are written
Not Te Deum ~
But to be read aloud
In the lyceum.
Those that aren't
Are meant to be
Buried in a mausoleum.

Fictionairy

<u>Hadj</u> < a journe
<u>Denji</u> < 'isle' in Singasling dialect (!?!)
<u>Hafazah</u> < a guardian angel
<u>Dhowrecked</u> < a wrecked dhow, probably because water got thru the w
<u>Lagan</u> < 1. cargo cast overboard in a storm 2. the booty from a naufrage
<u>Masoretic</u> < pertaining to the notes of the 10th C. scribes
<u>Pseudepigrapha</u> < 1. 'books' wrongly imputed to biblical authorships   2. misspelling of the word 'pseudography'
<u>Qumrām</u> < Dead Sea Scrollery
<u>Collegialism</u> < the separation of kirk from king
<u>Catachresism</u> < the -ism of abused words
<u>Shahada, Prayer, Sadaqa & zakat...</u> < please consult your local Imām

Sandzabaar, for the benefiction of those who ne'er hadj, is a nomadic crescent-shaped isle ~ a lopped off denji of the hopping lei of Pollenesia. 'Tis where The Rainbow Man & his hafazah spent more time than he'd like to think about ~ waiting for the blueth bird to mend its wing, clipped during the fall. There he met the local denizens: three dhowrecked devouts who dubbed him 'Caliph' ~ mistaking the angel-flying airlander for either a holy man, a jinni, e'en a very wealthy merchant. A lagan of literature, pagan & otherwise, translated to him by the angel Keela-la, whiled away his sabbatical ~ the dhow was a library ship enroute to the Sultan of Singasling, a very well read man. At length, Keela-la's wing healed & she blew the three devouts on a flying carpet ride to their Kaaba. Another truth was revealed to him ~ Sandzabaar wasn't an isle at all. 'Twas a Fornian De-Sludge turtle, like those that hibernate in the sludge water near De Citi ~ & are also mistaken for islands. "I have to get it back," saith the angel, "& with it, I might as well take the likes of you."

Asking for & allowed to take back one book with him on the long flying turtleback ride to Fornia, the man chose the only one without illustrations or illuminations. The Bicch was still a fresh wormhole in his noggin.

"Calif," asks Keela-la of the airlander whom angelically it doesn't know by any other name, "why did you chose the Qur´ān o'er the Holy Bible? What was wrong with the cute one, the Vulgate by Saint Jerome? It used to be the official Latin Bible. Of course, the St. James one ~ the version with the most brown-nose dedication e'er written ~ is truly a piece of prose in *that* primitive language. Excluding, perchance, the bogus vernacular of their darling playwit ~ Wm. Shakes... Anyoway, he annoys me with all his made-up theatricks. I wonder why he was ne'er annointed ~ annotated I mean. Then again, there is so much to be read in the Septuagint & naturally the Apocrypha could use the help of a literate editor. I found the Torah, according to the Masoretic text, to be quite esoteric. Did I tell you it *was* upside down & backwards when I read it to you? Why do you suppose that the Pope thinks the 'hidden books' Pseudepigrapha? I think they shed new light on the ol' subject! 'Tis a pity no one takes the Dead Sea Scrolls seriously ~ yet. Qumrām literature adds a cant of new collegialism to the old misstudy of catachresism ~ hmmm?"

At times when this blueth bird gets footloose at the mouthing, Calif wishes he *had* fallen, instead of hopping on its shoddy shoulder wing. He reflects o'er his sojourn on Sandzabaar. Not much to recollect o'er, he concludes. *Derndang,* this turtle stinks like a dunghole ~ 'tis what he really thinks.

"You know, I should've ne'er read you *Moby Dick ~ The Whale* reminds me of The Great Black Umpthing & that big hunk is what got ya into so*sooo* much trouble!!! Thing wanted you to seek out & describe The 21 Wonders for its sake, it did! Thank The Gods you only wood-burned pictures of those things & the Bicch ate 'em ~ otherwise you'd be rawbone worm-fodder ~ do you know that, Calif?"

"What is truly a wonder?" asks Calif.

"'Tis a wonder that anything as poorly inked as *Quotations From The Works Of Mao Tse-Tung* ~ you remember, that little red one ~ is the biggest bestseller ever unsold! It's the biggest publisher's giveaway & least circulated book in The Universe! Of course, where you come from nobody *copies* a book. There's the original & that's it! What do ya intend to do when I get ya back, Calif?"

"Word-burn *another* book," he replies.

"What makes you think it's not going to get you in more trouble, huh? The last one you did made everything you wrote ~ *happen!*"

Calif thinks awhile before answering the blueth bird. *It* ~ doesn't like answers anyoway, knows he. "My next work isn't going to be *factionairy* ~ it's going to be *fictionairy*," broadcasts he to Keela-la.

"Now, there's a foreign concept on Fornia! & I suppose you're going to try & translate tales from the Qur´ān ~ which is teatotally untrans- lateable, like your Fornian lexicon!"

"There are no stars on Fornia, right?"

"Nope ~ what you guys got is a Disc, 'tisn't even starry looking from you'all's vantage point ~ shroudy as it is!"

"That's it, then," sums up Calif, "this place you call the 'Sphere' with all its 'glimpse of blueth' ~ which to us implies 'batty in the old noggin' ~ & the images & the mirages of this upsidedown dreamland make for a good word- burning story."

"No one will read it ~ or even make-believe it ~ they'll say you *glimpsed way too much blueth!*" chuckles the angel.

"'Tis an airlandic story," defends the Fornian "on another level perhaps." Calif recalls a vivid memory of the 'moon'. Sometimes a Disc, horn, sickle, nilth. He remembers that he touched it once with a feather ~ it didn't tickle. Calif eyes o'er at the 'sun' ~ the red-hot fireball so ablaze as to batblind anyone! O, the delectable Disc, he misses it so.

Keela-la asks the airlander, more out of boredom than curiosity, "What are you going to call your next book?"

"Book?! ~ *you mean a book should be called something?*"

"Sure, it goes by the calling of 'title'."

"Hey, I like that concept. I, I will dub my new handuscript 'Five Pillars' ~ or something," the man proclaims, altho unsure.

"Let me guess the chapters," wordplays the angel, "1)Shahada, 2)Prayer, 3)Sadaqa & zakat & 4)Fasting!!!!"

"That's *only* four chapters!" protests Calif.

"A pilgrimage to Mecca isn't going to playout on Fornia!" announces Keela-la.

"Bird," relates the airlander, "you read to me how the Armymen rode a rock to the 'moon' ~ worthless as it is! If *they* can cross such a distance sitting on *their* arses, a short walk can not be beyond the realm of FORNIAN possibilities. I *once* walked from De Citi to El Lay & back!!!" Calif shows signs of being quite indignant.

The angel realizes the man is hard of listening & tries to change the subject. "What will you do if no one wants to read from your next book?"

"I'll push it off The Ledge-Edge where *your* favorite sect of people live & hope it falls on one of 'ems noggin!" threatens he.

The angel sighs at the last remark & states, "I don't think The Gods would like that very much! Besides, you can't count on me always flybying 'round these backspace parts of The Universe."

Calif, flipping channels, asks, "Do you think The Haggard Woman will be waiting for me to return?"

"The Haggard Woman?!" Keela-la stumbles & then mumbles, "oh, you mean *Shewn!* Maybe, if you'd shut up long enough for me to get you there."

"ME!, HUH," he huffs.

The Symphony of Silence intervenes for a long wingflap between the angel & the airlander atop the slumbering turtle.

"Mind if I dump this hefty De-Sludger first?" Keela-la asks.

"Not at all, I miss riding on your shoulder."

"We're almost there, hang on ~ it's going to make a mighty big splash."

"Wow, there's De Citi!!!"

zszszszszszszszszszszs spplASH!!!

"Where you want to be dropped off, Calif?"

"Anywhere, I know these parts."

"Calif, before I go, have you any messages for The Gods?" queries the angel Keela-la.

"Umpth ~ I will always choose *Life* o'er *Death* & *Death* o'er *Indifference.* Ta-ta!"

<u>*the end*</u>